Witch of the Crimson Coven

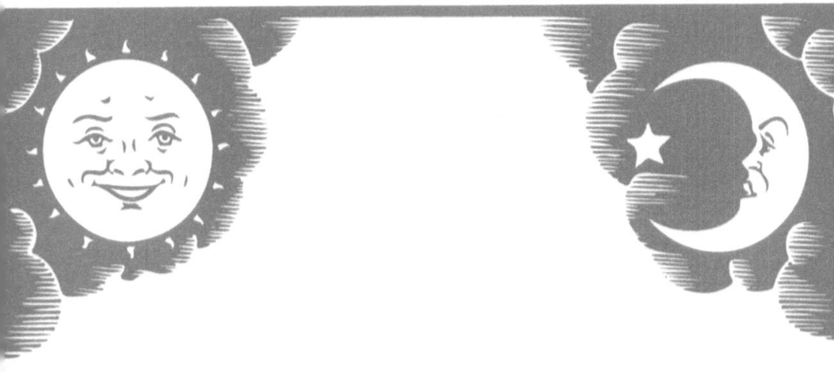

Witch of the Crimson Coven

DAWN OF THE BLOOD WITCH BOOK 6

Maria DeVivo

4 Horsemen
Publications, Inc.

Dedication:

For Babaysh—I appreciate your brain. You make this so much fun.

For Donna—Thanks for letting me kill you.

For Morgs—It's always for you, and always will be for you.

Table of Contents

Chapter One

Friday, April 2nd 1965
US Highway 40
Harmony, Indiana
Night of the New Moon

The brake lights on the Cutlass flicker their four red lines as it veers over to the side of the road. In the darkness, I can't tell if it's black or dark blue, but I know for a fact what type of car it is—an Oldsmobile Cutlass, just like my foster dad has. It had sped by us so quickly; I was shocked that the driver even saw us with our thumbs out. This stretch of Highway 40 isn't well lit, and the misty rain starting to fall has gotten me all panicky-like that I was willing to jump in the backseat of any ole goober's car.

I fold my distended thumb back into my palm and motion for Cyrinda to pick up the pace. She's been dilly-dallying for the last hour or so, and I've just about had it with her lackadaisical attitude. I mean, she wanted to jet outta town just as much as I did…

"C'mon!" I command against my gritted teeth.

She puts some pep in her step and reaches me before I take off at a serious trot toward the stopped vehicle under the streetlight. "Slow down," she whines, but I ignore her.

I secure my yellow duffle bag over my shoulder and hold the strap with a strong grip. I've never hitchhiked before, so I'd be lying if I said I wasn't a little antsy. As I approach the car, the driver rolls the window down, and I prop my elbows up on the ledge. The man smiles at me, and his brown eyes are like two magnified marbles behind his small, round glasses. He's greasy looking, and a waft of cigarette smoke billows out from the area around his seat making my stomach do a subtle somersault. But I'm grateful he stopped because we hadn't had any prospective rides in a while.

"Hey, Mister. Thanks for stopping!" I say. I move my body a little closer, so my head peeps into the car some more. I inspect the vacant backseat to verify that he is alone. Except for a plastic Tot-Guard in the back and some empty beer bottles on the floor, it's only him.

"Where's a pretty girl like you headed on a dark night like tonight?" he purrs. I pick up on his Southern accent, and a little quiver blossoms up on my forearms with goosebumps. He's not very handsome. Actually, as I move a bit closer to him, I see his bottom teeth are stained like he'd been sucking on chewing tobacco from the womb. Gross. Cyrinda stands behind me looking over my shoulder, and I know she's inspecting every last detail of the car as I had. Rightfully so, I mean, we are in this together, so…

I point at my chest, then motion to Cyrinda. "Oh, we're just headed a few towns over. Can ya spare us a few miles?"

The man looks me over and cocks his head to the side as if to get a glimpse of Cyrinda in the dim light of the streetlamp. He pushes his shaggy hair out of his eyes, squints a little, then smirks. "Sure. Sure, I can," he says with a long, drawn-out drawl. "How many towns were you thinkin'?"

I feel Cyrinda freeze in her tracks, and I look over my shoulder to gauge her facial expression. Her blue eyes are wide and wild, as if she's screaming to me from her insides saying, *No! Not this one!* I scan her face, my eyes darting back and forth over every inch of her expression like I'm trying to read what each word of her features says.

"Ummm…" I hesitate, still focused on Cyrinda. She wiggles her nose like Samantha on that show *Bewitched*, and that's my cue that it's a "no" for her—that she doesn't feel safe in this situation.

I silently mouth, "You sure?" and she gives a quick head nod. I take my elbows off the windowsill and step back from the car. "Yeah, um, I think we're just gonna walk for a little bit longer. We got some girl stuff to talk about is all and…"

"But it's gonna start raining hard!" he pleads. "C'mon, sugar, just get in. I'll take ya wherever you want to go."

Cyrinda tugs on my jacket at his insistence. "No really. We appreciate you stopping, but we're gonna change our plan up a tad," I say in my most gracious voice, trying to mask the jolt of terror that suddenly washes over me.

He scowls, but it's an expression born more from confusion than anger. "Oh well. Suit yourself. Just tryin' to help ya out." And with that, he peels out of there.

"Jesus, Cyri!" I yell into the night sky. "I mean, I know he was kinda scuzzy, but he was harmless! Did you not see the baby seat in the back?"

"I'm sorry!" she wails back, and her blonde bob bounces up and down on her forehead. "But we agreed! If either one of us got the heebie-jeebies we would hang back and wait for the next one."

"The next one? It's been forever for *that* one! You declined the one before that, and the one before that. Who does it have to be? Jesus Christ himself? Now we're gonna get caught in the rain, and…"

Just as I say it, the sky opens up drenching us from head to toe.

"Oh, Trixie!" she whines again. "I'm sorry! I'm so, so sorry!"

I pull my jacket up and over my head to try to keep my hair dry, and we walk away from the open lanes of traffic further back to the tree line and huddle close together.

"Do you think we should go back?" she asks.

"Home?" I roar, and she nods fervently. "No! Why would you say that? Do *you* want to go back to *that*? I mean, we agreed. There's nothing good coming out of there. There's nothing for us."

She hangs her head low with despair. Her sandy blonde locks are shaggy in front of her eyes, and I know she's trying to hide her tears from me. I know she doesn't want me to see her moment of doubt and second-guessing. She *always* second-guesses. Always. Ever since we were little kids playing on the playground together, I would be the first one to jump off the slide, and Cyrinda would be the one to question whether or not a fall could cause mortal damage or not. Sometimes I wondered why she and I were still friends—I mean, jeez Louise! She was such a scary Mary; it was often painful to be around.

"How are we ever going to know anything different from that place if we don't try?" I ask, but I think it's like the eleven hundred millionth time I've said it.

"I know, I know," she relents.

"We just gotta get to St. Louis," I say, repeating the plan. "Get to St. Louis, get some stupid jobs, find a place to hang our hats…"

"And just blend in with the city and no one will find us," she finishes the mantra.

"Exactly, my friend! And that's even if anyone comes looking for us."

We're shoulder to shoulder, and I feel her body tense up at my words. "You don't think they'll look for us?"

"Does it matter? Kids run away all the time. Besides, they'll probably be glad we're gone. I doubt they'll even notice right away."

She shivers, and it's not all from the rain.

I lean in closer to her ear, hoping my close proximity will comfort her and ease her hesitations. "You're second-guessing again," I say.

"Maybe," she answers sheepishly.

"But deep down, you know this is for the best. We're together. We're away from all the bullshit. We're gonna be strong and independent women! We're gonna make all our dreams come true, Cyrinda. You know it just as much as I do."

"How are you not scared?" she whispers, and the desperation in her voice practically breaks my heart. The poor thing. Always so meek and soft-spoken. Timid and shy. My sweet childhood friend—Cyrinda, the fragile little bird.

"What the hell makes you think I'm not scared? I'm as scared as a cat in a room filled with rocking chairs!" This is actually pretty spot on cause the rain, the dark, and all the prospects of the unknown are pretty damn frightening when I stop to think about it all.

"Coulda fooled me," she retorts. "You didn't seem so scared when that guy pulled up! Well, gee, you were alright and ready to hop on in the front seat and practically jump his bones!"

"Cyrinda!" I yell, swatting at her arm. "How dare you insinuate that I..."

"Well, if not that, then what?"

"Pray tell, how long have we been walking with our thumbs high in the air? And how many times has someone pulled over for us? Or rather, how many times have you declined the ride for whatever A, B, or C reason?"

She moves away from me, putting some distance between us. "C'mon, Trixie, you can't deny that guy was one scary looking man."

I shrug defensively, helplessly. "No, no, you're right. I'm not arguing that point. But the one before him?"

"Hippie."

"And the one before him?"

"Too old. Like a spooky grandpa."

I cover my head with my hands and groan in frustration. She's not understanding me.

"Trixie, we agreed! If we get weirded out, it's a no-go."

"Okay. Okay. How many times do I have to say you're right? You're right. We're in this together. Always. We stick together. Always. I mean, we've been best friends since we were like, what? Two years old? Something ridiculous like that! I think it's safe to say we're stuck with each other, hon."

She giggles softly like the little huffing pants of a miniature dog. The subdued sound of it makes me smile, and I move closer to her and put my arm around her shoulder.

"I was eager to get in that car because I was nervous. If we don't get a ride, we'll be walking all the way to St. Louis, and I don't want that to happen."

"Yeah, well, I'd rather walk all that way than get chopped up into little pieces by some creep."

I raise my eyebrows. "Deal. But you do know people hitchhike all the time, right?"

"Yeah, and people go missing all the time, Trix."

"Um, isn't that what we're trying to do though?"

Her shoulders relax a little, and she kind of melts into the crook of my arm. "Okay, but don't be so gung-ho about the next car that pulls up. Let's take our time. Really feel them out. And we both sit in the back."

The rain lets up, and I let go of my grip on her. "Sure," I say and nod for extra reinforcement. "We gonna get back out there, or are we walking to St. Louis?" I tease.

She giggles again and puts her hands behind her back in an innocent gesture. Immediately, my thumb pops out from my fist, and I trot back over to the dark stretch of highway.

It feels like only seconds pass when the Chevy Impala pulls over. I turn to Cyrinda and raise my eyebrows. "Alright, let's check this one out!"

She slumps her shoulders forward and hesitates, but she follows close behind nonetheless.

"Hey, thanks for stopping," I say with a touch of desperation in my voice when I approach the driver. "Not sure when that rain is gonna start up again."

The window was already down when he stopped, which for a split-second strikes me as odd, but I shake it off when I take in the full view of his face. He sure is something to look at! The rays of the streetlight catch the perfect angle of his chiseled jaw, accentuating his face with perfectly drawn shadows. I estimate he's in his late twenties, early thirties, and his smile is wide and bright just like a movie star's. There's a certain magnetism to it, and I can't help but be pulled in. Like Elvis but more rugged with some stubble about his chin and cheeks and his dark hair slicked back. Strangely, when our eyes meet, I can't decipher their color, but I chalk it up to the darkness. "Been out here long?" he asks, and his voice is melodic, soothing. The sound of it sends little pinpricks to the backs of my ears—they beg for him to keep talking, to keep filling them with his song.

Cyrinda snakes her head around me to check out what's going on in the backseat of the car, and she gives me the thumbs up to let me know he's alone. I smile. "A little bit. Not too long."

"Where ya headed?" he asks.

I move to the side and turn my head in Cyrinda's direction to include her in the conversation. "East of here. St. Louis?"

"Hmmm…" he drones and dips his head closer to the open window. "That sounds like more of a question than a statement. You sure that's where you wanna go?"

"Oh, definitely sure," I respond. The misty rain starts to intensify again, and I quickly look at Cyrinda to see how she's feeling about this one. She gives a quick head nod.

The man tilts his head up to the sky and examines the dome above. "Well, if you're getting in, best be now. Rain's gonna pick up any second."

Quickly I open the back door and Cyrinda hops in. Just as I'm about to follow after her, he says, "Whoa, whoa, whoa! Come sit up front with me. You're gonna make me feel like a chauffeur or something being in the back like that."

Cyrinda eyes me with a panic-stricken look. A look that says, *"Don't break our pact, Trixie!"* But I can't help it. I'm kinda feeling warm and fuzzy for this guy, and I can't put my finger on why. I slam the door behind her, jog over to the front passenger side, and slip into the front seat just as the sky opens up with its downpour. I can feel Cyrinda's eyes boring holes into the back of my head, but I ignore her intense stare down.

"So," he says in a suave voice as he puts the car into drive, "who do I have the pleasure of riding with tonight?"

I think my cheeks go pink. "I'm Patricia," I say sheepishly, and I thumb my finger to the backseat. "And that's Cyrinda. We're best friends going on an adventure of sorts, you can say."

The man nods at me and adjusts the rearview mirror so he can get a better look at Cyrinda. He squints his eyes and furrows his brow because she curls her knees to her chest and practically hides her face.

"She's the shy one, in case you couldn't tell," I whisper playfully, and she kicks the back of my seat.

"Sure, sure," he says. "Totally. I get it."

"And you are?" I press.

"Oh, people call me lots of things," he says as he accelerates onto the highway. The car lurches forward, and I instinctively grab the car door handle. "You know how that goes... *Trixie.*" His voice lowers with a sinister tone as he puts a weird emphasis on my name, and my stomach does a little lurch forward.

"H… h… how?" I stammer.

He gives me a side smile. A knowing smile. My nerves start to get the best of me, and I try not to turn my head to meet Cyrinda's face in the back. I know she's completely freaking out right now. "My real name is Patricia, but everyone calls me Trixie."

"Well, yeah," he says with a laugh. "It's so obvious! I mean, I don't think I've ever met a Trixie in my life before."

My muscles relax, and I let out a sigh of relief. I can feel Cyrinda ease up in the backseat, as well. "My mom was a big *Honeymooners* fan, but my dad wanted a more traditional name for me, so they agreed on it as a nickname."

He nods.

"So, where are you going?" I say, hoping to avoid a moment of awkward silence.

"As far west as west will go."

"California?" I crow, mystified.

"Something like that." He smirks his side smirk, again.

A glorious thought pops into my head. If he is going all the way out there, then… "Well maybe Cyrinda and I…" I blurt.

"Nope," he cuts me off, "you said St. Louis, and that's as far as I agreed to take you. Besides, where I'm headed is not the place for you. You don't need to get mixed up in any of *my* bullshit."

I giggle, but Cyrinda shifts uncomfortably in the backseat.

"You sure St. Louis? Where did you start out anyway? Indianapolis?"

I nod excitedly like a puppy dog. My blonde hair wisps in my face, and I quickly gather it to the side and let it flow down one shoulder.

"Silly. Trading one big city for another. If you really want to get away, really want to have an adventure, I'd go out to one of the smaller towns. No one would ever find you that way. But what do I know?"

"Like where? It's not like we have a map or anything. I wouldn't have the slightest idea where to go."

His right-hand releases from the wheel and he reaches over to change the radio station. The back of his hand brushes up against my knee and I flinch. His hand is unusually cold, like a block of ice swiped by me. He notices something transpire between us, too, because he smiles wider this time—his mouth opens so big that each one of his perfect white teeth are visible. The streetlights and car lights glint off them like some weirdo circus sideshow. The lights from the road make his face look jiggedy and jaggedy, and when I stare harder at him, I think I see a faint red X emblazoned on his forehead. I blink rapidly, trying to adjust my eyes to the strobing effects of the highway lights.

Suddenly, I'm overcome with the feeling that I've made a grave mistake. Suddenly, I fear I've led Cyrinda and me into an awful predicament, but the sensation is odd in my brain and in my heart and in the tingling in my fingers. I should be afraid—I *am* afraid—but there's an invisible blanket covering me, protecting me. It makes me feel fuzzy. Disconnected. Like what's happening in the car isn't really happening. I think I might just be tired or maybe it's my adrenaline working overtime. Like, us taking off with just a duffle bag full of clothes and some money in my pocket, sneaking out into the dark, hitchhiking in some handsome stranger's car—all of it—it's really needled its way into my consciousness.

"I'll get you where you wanna go," he says, as if reading my mind.

Cyrinda nudges my seat with her knee, and I clear my throat. "You never did tell me your name," I say with caution guarding my voice.

"Oh, Trixie," he sighs playfully, "where ever are my manners? I'm Trent."

Chapter Two

Friday, April 2nd 1965
North State Highway 49
Yale, Illinois
Night of the New Moon

Trent had turned up the volume on the radio, and a song blared out with which I wasn't familiar. It was a melodic song—one with a steady drum beat and some broads singing in perfect harmony together. He hummed and sang a few words here and there, and when I questioned him about the name of the song, or the band who made it, he ignored me, and went right on humming and singing. It was pretty (even if I couldn't really make out the words the ladies were saying), and I wanted to remember it so I could pick up that record once Cyrinda and I are settled in St. Louis. It annoyed me that he wouldn't tell me! He just held up one finger, as if to say "Wait 'til it's over."

And that was the last thing I remembered. It was like his voice and the sound of the music kinda lulled me into sleep. I passed out hard and fast! I mean, I was really tired after hitching all day, so that could have been a part of it too.

Trent hits a pothole in the road, and it jostles me awake. Cyrinda is out cold in the backseat, and the radio is off. I rub my eyes and stare out the window trying to make sense of my surroundings.

"How long was I asleep for?" I ask, my throat dry and groggy.

"About an hour," he answers matter-of-factly.

"An hour? Where in God's green earth are we?"

"Yale, Illinois. We just turned off I-70."

"Yale, Illinois?" I repeat. "Isn't that off the beaten path to St. Louis?"

"Eh," he says with a shrug. "Not too far off. I just need to make a pit stop at my…"

My body tenses up, and I draw my knees up to my chest. "Y… you never said anything about a pit stop!" I flail my arm to the backseat, hoping to hit Cyrinda and wake her up, but she's lying down, spread out across the seat in a deep, deep slumber.

"Relax, relax," he coaxes. "It's not a big deal. I told you I would take you to the city, and I will. I just have a little errand to run on the way. It's not a big deal."

"No man! Cyrinda and I…"

Trent narrows his eyes and adjusts his rearview mirror to get a look at Cyrinda in the back. He squints a little (Who knows? Maybe he needs glasses or something.) Hard at first, but then his eyes slowly open wide like something has dawned on him. He turns his attention back to me. "She's your shadow, isn't she?" he asks as if he's had some divine revelation.

Me and my shadow. Like that Mills Brothers song my foster mom used to sing around the house: *Me and my shadow…*

"Strollin' down the avenue?" Trent says, finishing the next line of the song. I flinch cause there's no way he could have known. That would mean that he read my mind!

"She holds you back, doesn't she?" he says, and it's more of a statement than it is a question.

"Cyrinda?" I squawk. "What ever do you mean?"

"You're in debt to her." He pauses. "No, that's not right. You take care of her."

"We take care of each other," I declare.

"But you feel bound to her. Obligated. Don't you."

I grip my knees tighter as the anger swells hot in my chest. "Look, man, you don't know anything about me and…"

He chuckles under his breath. "I know enough." He squints in the rearview again, back to me, then back to the inverted image of sleeping Cyrinda, and I know he's trying so hard to figure us out. He's trying so hard to figure out the dynamic between us—the who's, and why's, and when's, and where's. Trying to piece together the intricacies of our backstory. I could easily tell him how she and I met when we were little, how we helped each other through so many tumultuous and traumatizing situations, and how we wouldn't be alive today if it weren't for the other, but I refrain. He's a stranger. A stranger who isn't privy to those details. Those stories are for me and Cyrinda alone. There's a part of me that feels compelled to spill my guts, but I steel myself shut, and consciously go quiet.

The lights from the highway flicker again and reveal the color of Trent's eyes. They are gray—stormy and fierce. And when he looks in the mirror, when he looks at my sweet friend Cyrinda sleeping comfortably across the backseat one last time, there's a reflection in his eyes like a projector reel highlighting a recap of a movie: I see a child, and a river, and a bed, and a bathtub of blood, and…

I blink my eyes rapidly to rid myself of the images. "It's probably best if you don't talk to her. She's a nervous wreck. You'll just end up scaring her," I say, trying to pretend that I'm not afraid.

"Scaring her? You think she's afraid of me? Are *you* afraid of me?" he asks.

I pause for a second and take a deep breath. "No," I hesitate. "Yes," I say right after. "No and yes. Not of you, necessarily."

"You're running off adrenaline now, but when reality kicks in, so will the fear. The realist in you will take over."

"How do you know?"

"I know enough," he repeats. "Just how I know you're gonna sit there and tell me 'til you're blue in the face that you're twenty-one and that you got life all figured out. Or how you're not really running *from* something but running *toward* something."

I breathe in deep, letting my chest puff up as Cyrinda starts to stir awake in the back.

"How old are you, anyway?"

"Twenty-one…"

"Seventeen," he says at the exact same time as me, and I furrow my brow while he smirks in spite of himself. "Why did you leave Indianapolis anyway?"

"I don't really wanna talk about that."

"That's fine. That's fine. I understand."

Cyrinda sits up, reaches her arm over my side of the seat, and pets my hair. I grab her hand and squeeze tight, letting her know everything is okay. *I got this all under control.* I stretch out my leg, and at the same moment, Trent reaches over again for the radio. His hand makes contact with my knee, but this time he lingers there a little bit longer than our last physical encounter. He lingers there like his hand was lightning striking through the thick, blue fabric of my dungarees. There's a weird, electric charge that shoots straight up my thigh, and I recoil away from him before the feeling races to my brain.

Trent's eyes go black and wide. His pupils completely engulf the gray tones of his irises, and he sits at attention with both hands at ten and two on the steering wheel. Quickly, I turn the knob on the radio hoping some music will cancel out the awkwardness that has befallen us, but when the music crackles on, my face falls. *"Me and my shadow. Not a soul to tell our troubles to,"* The Mills Brothers croon.

Creeped out, I turn it off.

"You don't like that song?" Trent asks with a sarcastic tone.

"No," I say firmly, "I do. I just realized I was enjoying the quiet."

"Uh-huh," he mutters.

Cyrinda shimmies up closer to me. "Where are we going?" she whispers.

"Hey Trent," I say, trying to sound casual and friendly and not suspicious and abrasive, "where did you say we were going?"

"I told you; I need to run an errand at an old friend's place."

"Right. But where is that again?"

He chuckles. "It's on the way. I'll get you to St. Louis in no time, I promise."

I sigh with relief. I feel Cyrinda's hot breath on my hair as she sighs too.

"Unless..." his voice trails and he pauses. "Nah, forget it."

I cock my head to the side. "Unless what?" I ask.

"No, no, no," he says shaking his head. "Seems you got it all sussed out. St. Louis is the final destination. That is the master plan."

"So, what was the 'unless?'" I press.

He shakes his head harder, more dramatically. "Nope. Forget I said anything. We're about an hour out from where I need to go, and then about another two hours to your spot. It's fine. It's a good plan."

But his mannerisms and vocal inflection tell me otherwise. His tone fills me with doubt. The musical timbre of his voice gives me that dizzy, buzzy feeling in my head like it did before. I'm starting to feel like Cyrinda with all this doubting! Because I *did* have it all figured out!

I can no longer stand the suspense, so I beg, "Oh come on! If you have an alternative or something better, I'm willing to listen to it. It's not like I'm *not* open to suggestions. Give me three good reasons why we shouldn't go to St. Louis."

He inhales and exhales sharply like he's aggravated that I didn't figure this out on my own. "Well, for starters, like I said before, leaving one big city for another isn't the smartest idea. I understand you think you're going to blend in in St. Louis, but you're really not. You've had the protection of teachers and mentors and guardians and other adults in your life when you were in Indianapolis, but in St. Louis, people will sense your layers are pulled back. They'll spot your weakness a mile away."

"Go on."

"And then there's the issue of the basic necessities. Food? Shelter? Hygiene? Do you have a job lined up? Do you know anyone in St. Louis? Do you have friends you can stay with? Park benches are okay for a night or two, but that gets old real fast."

I pause, absorbing his words. That was something I had only thought about in passing. The plan was to use the money I had saved to stay in a cheap hotel while I secured a job. Then eventually we would get an apartment when the money started coming in. But what if it wasn't going to be that easy? "And three?"

"Well, that's the easiest one, Trixie. Girls get eaten alive in big cities. Especially virgins like you."

My face and ears get hot with embarrassment. "Hey! Hey!" I yell. "That is certainly not any of your business and…"

He holds up his right hand and makes a pressing down motion like he's pumping the brakes on the car. "Relax, relax," he says gently. "There's absolutely nothing wrong with being pure. It's actually quite noble. Too many gals are quick to jump in the sack with any guy who gives them an ounce of attention."

Cyrinda kicks the back of my seat, and I give her an angry, sideways glance.

"Like I said, you don't know me. You don't know anything about me," I huff indignantly and cross my arms over my chest.

"Oh," he says, the sarcasm dripping from his tongue. "I'm wrong?"

I nod furiously, but it's a lie. And he knows it. Sighing, I sink back into the car seat and think just how stupid and pathetic I really am. Poor little Trixie, a virgin at seventeen. Ran away from home to get away from her messed up, stupid life but dragged her best friend along the way and got them both into something they are probably never getting out of. Just great. Typical Trixie. Stupid, dumb, idiot, Trixie. Fucking things up once again.

If that isn't the story of my life!

I look back to Cyrinda and mouth, "I'm sorry," to which she shakes her head, as if to reassure me everything is going to be okay. Isn't *that* rich? Nervous Nelly Cyrinda telling *me* it's going to be okay! Man, I must have really crossed over into the *Twilight Zone*. At this point, it wouldn't surprise me if we saw Rod Serling himself hitch-hiking on the side of the freeway!

Trent puts his hand on my knee, and again, I feel that odd sensation course through my body. But this time, I don't pull away. I let it jolt me with what feels like an electric charge from my knee all the way up to the base of my skull. His touch leaves me breathless, speechless. My arms go numb, and it feels like a thousand spiders scuttle their way under my skin and up to my head. With their multitude of legs, they try to pry open the locked doors inside my brain—trying to get at me, poke at me, open me up, and read me like an insect book of forbidden fairy tales. The spiders are fuzzy and black, and they make *me* feel fuzzy and black, like I'm about to pass out or maybe pass away.

Luckily, Cyrinda kicks my seat, and I snap out of it.

Trent takes his hand off my leg and my vision slowly returns to focus.

"You're right. You're right. I don't know you, and it's not fair for me to presume to. But I know what you're feeling. I know something happened to you that was so bad that you felt compelled to run away. I get it. You're not the only one to ever feel like that or do something about it for that matter. But you gotta believe me when I say this: the world is a dangerous place. Especially when you're out there on your own. Trust me. I know. I've traveled the world over many a time, and there's one thing I've learned for certain. The world preys on young girls like you. Like sharks smelling blood in the water. And believe you me, they will smell your innocence coming a mile away. Especially those derelicts on the streets of St. Louis."

Cyrinda paws at my shoulder frantically, and I lean my head back to be closer to her. What Trent said freaked her out something awful. I'm not gonna lie, it got me spooked too. If we can't get situated right away and have to find a shelter or sleep in a park… I don't even wanna think about having to deal with the vagabonds and hippie drug addicts. We could get killed. Even worse, we could get raped.

"Ask him about what he was going to say before," Cyrinda whispers.

"Shhhhh," I say silencing her. "I got this! So, tell me, Trent. If you were in our situation what would *you* do?"

"Hmmm…" he ponders. "Look. The place I need to run the errand is at the home of a very old and very dear friend of mine. We haven't seen each other in what feels like ages."

I perk up. "Ohhhh! Old girlfriend?" I tease.

"Something like that," he answers. "She's not expecting me, and quite honestly, I hadn't initially planned on stopping there when I set out for California. And even though a lot of time has gone by since we last saw each other, we still have a strong bond."

"You've kept in touch with her over the years?"

"Something like that."

"Awww," I say excitedly, swatting at his thigh. "She's your love! I can totally tell! Are you planning on getting back together with her?"

Trent glares at me from the corner of his eye for a scary second, and I bite my lower lip to prevent myself from gushing anymore. "Anyhow," he finally continues, "this friend of mine is very welcoming. She's known to help out young girls in trouble. There's a soft spot in her heart for helping others. Runaways. She was a runaway herself once, but unfortunately, she didn't have anyone to help her, so she made it her business to help those in need. She's very warm and loving. Motherly-like. I really think you guys would get along swell."

The way he describes the woman touches my heart. Like, there's palpable emotion in his voice—a sadness, a deep respect, a love, a longing.

"Wow," I say sincerely. "That's neat. But how does it all work?"

"Simple. It's not like a shelter or anything. She goes about her business day to day, and if there's a girl who needs help, she'll find a way to help 'em out. She gives them a place to stay, helps them get a job, and gets them on their feet until they can get settled on their own. She has a group called The Sisterhood. It's for young ladies like you to bond and get empowered and all that girly stuff."

"Hmmm…" I say skeptically. "What's the catch?"

"No catch. Just help around the house. Be a team player. Actively look for a job. Cook a few meals…"

"Trixie can't cook!" Cyrinda blurts out, and I start giggling. Trent eyes me suspiciously again.

"Sorry, sorry," I apologize and quit laughing. "Go on."

"I don't know. You asked what I would do. Well, I would go there. To Barbara Thorne's. Let her take care of you until you can take care of yourself."

"Barbara," I sigh, repeating her name. It feels like a warm blanket across my shoulders on a crisp winter night—when part of my body is still blasted with cold air, but my upper torso is nice and snuggly. Her name sounds like hot cocoa and marshmallows. To say it out loud makes me comforted and safe.

Cyrinda reaches for my hand and squeezes tight. "Barbara," she whispers in my ear. Her voice is childlike and giddy, and I know she feels it too. She feels the same solace and serenity in her name alone. Cyrinda is excited at this new prospect, and for once I, too, am seeing a painting of a bigger picture that does not include the flashing lights of the big city. Alas, I was wrong. *Again.* But I'm starting to think that Trent might very well be our savior if he can set us up with his Barbara.

"I think you're right, Trent. Cyrinda and I would probably do much better there than in St. Louis. She sounds like an extraordinary woman." I don't want to say her name again because it feels like a spell, and I'm afraid I'll wake up from a pleasant dream only to find us on the streets of downtown St. Louis. I don't want the idea of Barbara to fade away. I need her to be real.

"Oh, she most definitely is." He smiles wide at the thought of her, and I swear I think a red X flickers on his forehead for a second.

"So, where is this place? Where does she live?"

"Well, it's now about a half hour away. Salem, Illinois."

"Salem?" I giggle nervously. "Is that like where the witches are?"

"Something like that."

Chapter Three

Friday, April 2nd 1965
Barbara Thorne's House
163 North Shelby Avenue
Salem, Illinois
Night of the New Moon

The sky is black as pitch—a dome of endless darkness, save for the stars that litter the atmosphere. With no moon to be seen, the stars are like lost children scattered throughout the universe, flickering, and sputtering what little light they have. Like a thousand illuminated beacons calling out to their Mother Moon to come home to them.

With barely any streetlights, it's hard to make out any of the buildings and structures until the headlights of the car are right up on it, and then it goes by so fast that I can't seem to make heads or tails of anything out there in the world. But I can make out the lightning trees lining the streets— big, hulking trees that have been struck one too many times and are barren and bare. They are scarred by the energy they absorbed and left hollowed out on their insides. Like monsters with tree limbs for arms, they hover over the houses in a protective stance.

I don't know why I think these things as Trent drives through the town, but I get an urgent sense that we are getting closer to our final destination. I feel Cyrinda perking up in the back. She looks longingly out the window and sighs ever so often.

I barely register the street sign when Trent makes a right-hand turn down North Shelby Avenue because out of the right-hand passenger side view, even in the moonless darkness, even with the scattered stars trying hard to shine their lights upon the world, I am met with a grim sight—the entire right-hand side of the street is what appears to be miles upon miles of headstones.

A twinge inside me panics. Is this some sick joke? Was the Barbara and peace and comfort Trent spoke so highly of just a code for cemetery? Is Trent planning on killing us and putting us in that cemetery?

He chuckles a little, and I swear to God I know this man is reading my mind somehow. He has to be. It's too freaky how he gestures, mutters, or chuckles right in time with my stream of consciousness.

"I… is… is Barbara dead?" I stammer.

"What?" he crows. "Why would you say that?"

"Um… the graveyard?"

"Oh please, Trixie. Don't be so silly. Barbara lives *across* from the cemetery, not *in* the cemetery!"

Cyrinda *phews* in the back.

"This is kinda creepy, though. Don't cha think?" I ask him, looking for some kind of reassurance that my creep-o feelings are justified.

"Think about it," he says, "the only neighbors you have are the ones next to you. The people across the street aren't giving you too many problems now are they?"

"Unless they haunt you," Cyrinda says flatly.

I let out a giggle.

"Huh?" Trent inquires, and I know he didn't hear her.

I wave my hand in the air to dismiss it. "Nothing, nothing."

"Eastlawn Cemetery is a perfectly peaceful place. Yes, there are lots of headstones, but it's rather quite serene. A wonderful place to meditate, center yourself, cleanse your spirit... I know Barbara chose this area to settle into because it's quiet and..."

"Contemplative," I finish for him. I don't know why I blurted that, but the word just kinda popped into my head as Trent was pulling over on the side of the road where the houses were lined up.

"Exactly," he cheers. "I couldn't have said it better."

The house he pulls up in front of is a white shingled, two-story home with red trim around the three front windows, and a red door.

Like blood, I think to myself, but shake my head so the thought flies out of my brain and up into the night sky.

"This is it," he says as he puts the car in park. "This is Barbara's place."

We all pause when no one makes a move to exit the car, and I shoot him a questioning look. "Aren't you… I thought you said you had an errand to run? That's why you were coming out this way. Aren't you going to get out and run that errand?"

"Oh, it's done. I did it already," he answers cryptically.

"O… oh," I stutter again, not understanding what he meant. "You're not gonna get out with us? Walk us to the door?"

"Nope. This is your drop-off. You'll be fine."

"O… okay," I say, and the hesitation in my voice is near deafening to me. "You're not gonna come up and see your friend, at least?"

"No. It's not time for all that yet. But please tell her I sent you." He puts his hand on my knee and looks directly into my eyes. In his, I see gray clouds across the horizon, and I think I smile. "Tell her Galen sent you."

"Galen?" Cyrinda wails.

"You said your name was Trent," I say with an accusatory tone.

"It's an inside joke we have," he answers with a slick smile. "Tell her both. It'll be her way to fully believe you."

I nod like a puppy dog, and Cyrinda clicks open her door and scampers over to the front door.

"Trixie, you're gonna be right as rain." He winks at me, and the clouds in his eyes open up and a gentle mist sweeps the horizon of his pupils.

I turn my upper body and open the door. "Thank you," I say. "You really helped us."

"Nah. Nothing to it. Just remember to keep your good thoughts flowing and your actions to match!" He flashes me his pearly whites. His pearly whites set in his perfect mouth on his devilishly handsome face with the red X on his forehead, and as I step out of the car and real rain blurs my vision, I look back to the car to catch a final glimpse of our ride, but I can't seem to make him out. Like, I couldn't see his face through the windshield as we jogged in front of the car, but that could just have been the darkness and the raindrops making him look so damn fuzzy—like he's not a real person or something.

Like he was never even there.

I catch up to Cyrinda and ring the bell as Trent pulls away in a hurry. I watch as the car vrooms down the avenue until I can no longer see the taillights. He's long out of sight before someone finally answers the door.

The rain starts to come down harder, and Cyrinda shivers behind me. She tugs gently on the strap of the yellow duffle bag flung over my shoulder. I reach my hand behind my back to signal to her: *We're okay. We can do this.* The red door swings open with fury and the person on the inside of the house narrows her eyes defiantly at me. She's a tall young woman with broad shoulders and short black hair cut in that popular Twiggy hairstyle. I have to do a double take at first because in the dim light, and from behind the mesh of the screen door, I initially mistake her for a boy. "Can I help you?" she barks with the ferocity of a wild animal, but her voice lilts with a high-pitched femininity that doesn't seem real coming from her mouth.

Thunder rumbles low in the night sky and I shudder from both the noise of the impending deluge and the aggressive nature of the girl at the door. "B… B… Barbara," I stutter in a weak voice. "We're here to see Barbara Thorne?"

The girl eyes me up and down, looks over my shoulder at Cyrinda, and crinkles her nose. She lets out a little huff, and defeated, I start to turn my body to descend the steps and out into the vast nothingness of this unfamiliar town. *We've been played*, I think. *Tricked*. Cyrinda slumps her shoulders forward in defeat and lets out a long sigh. "Plan C," I say to her with fake confidence as the swell of fear and anxiety once again rises to my throat. I try desperately to push it back down, so it doesn't leak out of my eyes. 'Cause if I start crying now, I'm not sure I'll be able to stop.

But soon another woman comes to the door, like she magically materialized at the side of the androgynous woman, and a glowing light dances around her. Suddenly, I am overwhelmingly entranced. I stop in my tracks to stare at her beauty. Her glory. Her complete and utterly pulsating aura. Cyrinda turns around as well, and she stares in awe. I don't have to be formally introduced to know who the woman is—when Trent described her to me, this was the vision I had in my head, right here, right now, in the dim light of the street and from behind the mesh screen door. Another type of feeling swells in my chest—a feeling of safety and comfort, like how I felt when Trent spoke of her.

Barbara.

"Ronnie, who's this?" she asks the girl with the stern face.

Ronnie shrugs her shoulders. "She said she was here to see you?"

Barbara looks at me as Cyrinda tries to conceal herself. "That right?" she asks.

"Yes, ma'am," I answer, and I feel so dumb after it leaves my mouth. Barbara isn't a "ma'am!" Ma'ams are old, stuffy women who wear solid-colored dresses and white pearls around their necks. Ma'ams twist their long, gray hair into tight buns on tops of their heads and look down their noses at you. Barbara is certainly not *that*—her long brown hair cascades over her left shoulder, and a black beret sits tilted to one side on her head. Her black and white striped shirt is tucked into tight-fitting black jeans, like the quintessential Beatnik woman. And her face! She is an absolute vision of beauty with porcelain doll-like features like they were hand-painted by the finest dollmaker and finished up with alabaster skin that bears no scar or blemish. Like straight out of a fashion rag or some high-end department store magazine. But it's not her clothes, or hair, or groovy vibe that makes me awe-struck. It's her light. The light that pulsates around her pulls me in like a magnet. I can't stop staring.

And I notice she stares right back at me. Her dark eyes flicker with an almost unnatural light like they're catching the glimmer of fireworks in the distance.

"What can I do for you?" she asks, and her voice is even more lovely than her face. I could listen to her speak forever. There's subtle music in her voice, like the soft notes of an ancient song playing in time with her words. And she continues to stare at me—uncomfortably, but not. Like she's searching for something on my face. Like she's trying to pinpoint something about me that feels, I don't know, almost familiar?

For a second I am lost in it all, and almost forget who I am, where I am, what I'm even doing here. Cyrinda nudges me to answer, and I snap out of my semi-trance. "Yes, um… I'm Trixie. This is Cyrinda," I finally say. "I was told you could help us."

"Well, that depends on who you've been talking to," she says playfully, and she and the other girl share an inside-joke chuckle that makes me feel alienated and alone.

"Trent," I blurt, and the two immediately silence their laughter. Barbara looks at me wide-eyed. Her face is like a stone statue frozen in time… actually, it's like her whole body is frozen in time at the sound of his name. And it's almost as if that vague familiarity she was trying to pin-point about me came crashing into full acknowl-edgment. "But he said you knew him as Galen? I don't know," I stammer, and I realize how stupid we must look and sound. "He brought us here. He said you could help us. He told us we would be safe."

Her eyes go round and wild. They are no longer black, but a gold hue, like honey. I blink rapidly because I suddenly can't remember if they were this color just a moment before. My own eyes must be playing stressful tricks on me…

"Trent? *Galen*?" she asks in disbelief, sounding out each word of his name as if she were in slow motion.

"Y… yeah. He said he was an old friend of yours and that you help girls like us. He told me that your house is like a sanctuary or something. Sisterhood? And when I asked him if he was going to come in to say hello to you, he said it wasn't time yet, or something." I hate that there's confusion and hesitation in my voice.

But a grin sweeps across her perfect face, and she opens the door wider, shoos Ronnie to the side, and welcomes us into her home. "Come. Come in. Come in. Get out of the rain, you poor thing." The tone of her voice and swiftness in her gestures have totally shifted.

Ronnie glares hard at us. At me. It's a suspi-cious look that I don't understand. Her eyes are hard and cold, and I know she's judging me—she's judging *us* as we walk past her and into the house. There's an instant feeling of friction between us, like two same-sided magnets trying to touch each other but not able to make a connection. It reminds me of school when the hard city girls who were bussed in from downtown gave me dirty looks in the hallway and rumors of fights "at the flagpole at 3 p.m." circulated every afternoon. I never did have a fistfight at school, but if this bitch wanted to start some beef, I was a-okay with that. The scent of patchouli oil wafts in my nose as I pass her by. She reeks of it like the hippies hanging out at the Ruins in Holiday Park—with their bandanas and tambourines and the occasional scent of reefer. But it's the patchouli that makes the hippies *hippies*. So gross. I roll my eyes at the smell of her. I ignore it and follow closely behind Barbara through the foyer and into the living room with Cyrinda right on my heels. "Thank you so much," I gush.

Barbara stops and turns to face me. She places her hands at my biceps and holds me tightly. A rush of cool energy engulfs me, and I feel like I'm sinking into the green plush carpet. Like I am weightless and not in control of my own self. I glance down as her long, black fingernails nudge their way securely into my armpits. "If Trent sent you, I can't deny you," she says, and her black eyes stare deeply into mine. They move quickly back and forth as if they are scanning me, looking for something, searching for something. I try to track their movements with mine, but she is too quick for me and soon breaks our stare.

"He touched you!" she says like she's pleased or something.

I stiffen up, confused. "He didn't… I didn't… no, it wasn't…"

"No, dear, I mean he *touched* you. Maybe on your arm, or shoulder, or your knee perhaps."

"Oh, yes. I mean, he might have brushed up against…"

Her eyes dart back and forth across my face. She scans me again, continuing her search for what I do not know.

"You've come a long way, haven't you?" she says.

I nod.

"And you're scared. You're trying so very hard not to be, but you are."

I nod again.

"Oh, sweetie," she sings sympathetically. "Someone hurt you. That's why you left. Someone hurt you really bad."

Didn't they, Trixie? Her voice booms in my head, and for the first time in a few days, the tears spring to my eyes—hot and uncontrollable. The red flush of embarrassment stings my checks as I quickly swat away at the stream. I know I'll get no comfort from Cyrinda because she's probably a bumbling, crying mess behind me as well, but Barbara digs her fingers into my arms, and I seem to forget Cyrinda is even there. Barbara's eyes suddenly stop their search, and they go wide like she's had some wild revelation.

She has October in her eyes. Fire and warmth and power, I think, but I don't know why that popped into my head.

"But not bad enough." Barbara winks. "You still have your innocence. And *that* is a blessing. That makes you glow." She takes my face in both her hands and wipes underneath my eyes with her unusually lengthy thumbs, pressing the sharp, prickly ridges of her black nails just underneath the bottom of my eye sockets. "Don't want the salt to burn your cheeks," she says, but I can't be sure if she actually said it out loud or not. "Come. We're wrapping up a Sisterhood meeting in the back room. Let me finish up with them, then we'll get you squared away." She interlocks her arm with mine and leads me down a narrow hallway.

The back room is a small den with what appears to be a thousand candles lighting the space. Three girls sit Indian style on the carpet in a circle formation. Barbara motions her hands for us to sit down with the group, and the girls shimmy their positions to make room. Ronnie stands like a sentry by the door, and Barbara enters the center of the circle.

"Sisters," she says, raising her arms high above her head. "As we conclude this New Moon ceremony, let us reflect upon the intentions and energies we've invoked. The New Moon symbolizes a time of beginnings," she pauses and trains her eyes on me. The girls in the room turn their heads to look at me, and I can't help but blush. "It is a time of setting intentions, and of embracing change," Barbara continues, "and we have come together under the night sky to connect with the profound energy of the moon and the natural world."

Ronnie walks around the room and begins putting out all the candles.

"As we extinguish the candles and close the circle, we carry with us the wisdom, strength, and insights we've gained here. May the intentions we've set be nurtured and grow as the moon waxes, and may the seeds of our desires find fertile ground in the days and weeks to come." Barbara smiles at the group in the darkness.

The three girls in the circle rise and embrace Barbara. She kisses them on each cheek and bids them farewell. When the last of the candles is extinguished, Ronnie walks the three out of the room, and I assume, out of the house. Cyrinda and I stand up and follow Barbara down the hallway back towards the front door and into the kitchen where we all sit at the round Formica table.

"I run a group called the Sisterhood," Barbara explains. "It's where women come to gather and meditate and share philosophies and such."

"Trent never said anything about some hippie witchy stuff," I say bluntly. Cyrinda swats my knee under the table to shut me up.

Barbara laughs out loud, her voice like a tinkling bell on a cold winter night. It fills the room with its musical lilt and washes over my ears. "Oh no, not really. Those girls are just looking for an alternative to some spiritual guidance. A little smoke and mirrors never hurt anybody. If I can bring them a little bit of peace, then so be it. Besides, our little gatherings are very soothing. You might want to join us."

I shrug my shoulders. "They don't live here with you?"

"No. Just Rhonda."

"Is she like your what ... sister? Best friend? Cousin?"

Barbara huffs out a stifled giggle. "Ronnie's more of an associate, I guess you can say. She's helping me with something I'm working on. We all have our shadows, don't we?" She raises her right eyebrow, and I go cold on the inside for a second. "So, Trixie, if Galen brought you here, I will do whatever it takes to help you out. You have my word."

"It's that easy?" Cyrinda blurts.

"Easy as peach pie," Barbara reassures. "I'm sure Galen told you he and I go way back."

We nod simultaneously. "Why do you call him Galen?" I blurt, and this time Cyrinda kicks me. Hard.

Barbara ignores my question. "There's an extra room if you need to stay. Ronnie knows the manager at the movie theatre in town, and I'm sure she can try to set you up with some work."

We nod simultaneously, again. Barbara's words dance like a song in my head. Each individual letter twirls and swirls for each word. She's soothing and calm, not like the other adults in my life who speak with nothing but anger and violence and malice—trying to hurt me with their degrading and abusive words.

This can't be real. Are we finally safe? Are we finally in a place we can call home?

Ronnie comes stalking into the kitchen and eyes us coolly at the table.

"But I will ask something of you in return," Barbara says.

"Oh," I answer hesitantly. "What?"

Suddenly, Ronnie opens the refrigerator door, reaches inside, and pulls out a glass bottle of pop, and as she moves away to the side before closing the door, I get a full view of the contents within. Cyrinda sees it too, for she clasps my knee with a vice-grip. Inside are four large plastic cartons filled with bags. But not just any kind of bags—bags I'd seen before when I had to go to the hospital for my appendix surgery when I was nine. Bags that are filled with a deep, dark red substance that could only be one thing…

Blood.

A tiny gasp escapes my throat, and Ronnie quickly closes the fridge door.

Barbara folds her hands together on top of the table and leans in closer to us. "I'm going to need you to help me with something very, very special."

Chapter Four

Saturday, April 3rd 1965
Barbara Thorne's House
163 North Shelby Avenue
Salem, Illinois
Early Morning of the Waxing Crescent Moon

Of course, Cyrinda and I agree to what Barbara asks, even though she never fully did get into the specifics of the thing. But what she did convey to us was that this project she has in mind is totally important and that we will be doing really good work for a really good cause. After we talk for a little bit, Barbara takes a wine bottle from one of the cabinets and pours red wine into ornate goblets. (I only know it's called that because my foster mother was a right lush). The glass is thick with jagged ridges of heavy lead crystal. Cyrinda puts her hands up to refuse the drink, but I gladly accept.

Barbara gives me a side-smirk of approval and a quick wink of her eye. "It's only proper to have a small toast for new beginnings," she says as she raises her glass, and we all follow suit and clank them together. Cyrinda sneers at me in disapproval. She has never been one to even sneak a drink, so I'm not surprised.

The wine is sour with a slight metallic aftertaste, and I can't help but crinkle my nose when it goes down. It feels like liquid fire in my throat, and Barbara and Ronnie both laugh out loud. "It's from the old country," Barbara says, and she and Ronnie tap their glasses together again before chugging the last of their glasses.

"What country would that be?" Cyrinda asks in a rather obnoxious way that I sneer at her. Thankfully, Barbara and Ronnie both ignore it.

"Drink up!" Ronnie encourages me. "It's rude not to finish your host's offering."

I look deep into the glass before downing the last of the strange-tasting wine. I mean, I've had wine before, and I'm not saying I'm a connoisseur or anything like that, but this stuff is super grody. Old country or not, I didn't care for it at all. It is strong, too, 'cause I immediately feel it working its way into my head, giving me that slight head change or what my foster mom calls "a buzz."

Barbara then tells Ronnie to show us to our room. She says we can stay as long as we like, even after we help her with her special project (if we want).

The spare room Ronnie takes us to is next to the den where the Sisterhood meeting was held. The queen size bed is in front of a window that overlooks a decent-sized backyard. It's big enough for me and Cyrinda—besides, we've been together for god knows how many years that we usually end up sleeping next to each other during sleepovers and campouts and all that. I plop my body onto the bed, claiming my side, and sprawl out with a sigh. I anticipate a good night's sleep after all the excitement this day has brought, and my body already starts to mold itself into the mattress. Cyrinda joins me and rests her head against my shoulder. I know she's feeling the same way — the same sleepy, heavy-eyed feeling as me.

Ronnie walks over to the dresser in the corner and starts taking clothes out of the drawers. "Wait, wait, wait!" I exclaim, but my voice is groggy and thin. "Is this *your* room?"

"Not anymore," Ronnie answers. She doesn't look at me and continues pulling things out and folding them over her bent arm. "I'm moving out."

"Oh," I say with a little shock. "It's not because of us, is it?"

She swivels her head in my direction and glares at me hard. I can't tell if she's mocking me, or if she's giving me a "no, it's not" look. "I don't know if any of my stuff will fit you. You're kinda on the short side, ya know? But I'm totally willing to share. I'm just taking out what I really want, but that closet over there is filled with all kinds of stuff if you need anything."

"Thank you," Cyrinda mumbles.

The initial feelings I had when I first met Ronnie start to melt away like water poured over a snowball. I can only imagine what *she* must have felt when she opened the door to two strangers all disheveled in the rain at her doorstep. Her dirty looks and apprehension toward us was normal. I see that now. She speaks to me so casually, so friendly, that I feel bad for having thought she is bitchy and wants to kick my ass. The stark contrast of her sweet voice and her semi-masculine exterior fascinates me, and I panic a little at the thought that she's going to leave the house before I get a chance to figure her out. "Are you leaving?" I ask as I prop my body up on my elbows.

"Nope. Just switching rooms."

I exhale quietly and relax my body back against the pillows. I kinda don't want her to go—she's intriguing to me, and there's something about her dynamic with Barbara that I need to figure out, so I try to pry a little and engage her in conversation. "How long have you lived here with Barbara?" I ask, and I realize that when I say her name out loud, it makes me feel warm and in a dreamlike state.

Ronnie stops and looks up at the ceiling as if trying to mentally calculate time. "Hmmm. Let me see," and she mutters something unintelligible. "Hot damn!" she squeals, snapping her fingers. "It's been almost eight months!"

"Jeez Louise! That's a while."

Ronnie moves over and sits at the edge of the bed, and that excites me—makes me feel comfortable and at ease. She places the stack of clothing in her lap and gently rests her elbows on the pile. "Yeah. But I wouldn't change anything for the world. Barbara has been like my savior or something. She really helped me get my shit together and find my way."

Cyrinda twinges at Ronnie's use of profanity, and I swat her arm because I get a feeling from the way Ronnie says Barbara's name, she feels the same way about her too. My skin crawled when Barbara left us to retire to her room—it itched on the inside, like a junkie craving their next fix, like my actual flesh *needed* to be in her presence.

Ronnie shuffles a little, and I fear she's going to leave. "Can I ask you a question?" I say sheepishly.

"Lay it on me."

I pause for a few seconds debating whether or not I should actually ask her, but Ronnie's dark eyes beckon me to continue. They sparkle in their sockets like black gems against a lamplight. Crystalline like the volcanic glass I observed in my earth science class. "What's up with all the blood in the fridge?" I finally say in a low voice.

Cyrinda digs her short nails into my thigh as Ronnie's shoulders tense and her eyes open wide for a split second. "Blood? Oh, you mean the blood bags?"

"Yeah," I say with a nervous little chuckle. "I saw them when you opened the fridge and it's… I don't know… kinda weird?" I try to choose my words delicately, so it doesn't come off as offensive to my host.

She laughs. "Oh, it totally is! I work for the medical center in town. One of their refrigerators went down, so they asked all the workers to take some bags home until they could get it back up and running."

I squirm. "Creepy."

"Yeah. Not the most ideal situation to have bags of people's blood in your house." She laughs again. "Look, like Barbara said, I know the manager at the movie theatre." She changes the subject so nonchalantly that I scarcely notice she's completely shifted gears. "If you wanna go up there in the morning, I can introduce you and see if you can start working as soon as possible. I've gotten plenty of girls a job there. The manager is a real scummy old guy and is only looking for pretty girls to work for him, but the pay is good and the hours are decent, and it's easy enough work, and…"

"Sure," I say, cutting her off. "I'm in." I pause. "*We're* in."

"Groovy," she says and gives me a peace sign. She gets up from the bed and walks over to the door, clothes in hand. "Barbara sees something in you, you know. I don't know what it is, but it's definitely something special. She doesn't normally just take anyone in."

"Far out," I say and nod my head proudly.

"How do you know Galen anyway?"

"Well, he told us his name was Trent, and I don't know him at all. He was just our ride. We hitched with him."

"Yeah," she says almost dreamily, "but you got to *meet* him."

"Why does she call him that when he told me his name was Trent?"

Ronnie shrugs her shoulders. "I dunno. She gets real dicey when she talks about him. They go back a long time. Like, long ago type of shit. I've never met him. Only heard her stories about him." She pauses for a second as if she's imagining him. "What exactly did he say to you?" she asks, and the pitch of her voice rises with excited curiosity.

I shrug my shoulders like a dummy. "I dunno. A bunch of stuff. Weird stuff. He told me to keep my good thoughts flowing…"

"And your actions to match," she says in time with me. The three of us laugh. "I've heard a lot of Trent stories—*Galen* stories. Apparently, he and Barbara were like…"

"Going steady or something?"

"Yeah. That's the feeling I got. I think Barbara still has it bad for him."

I sit up fully erect. "Exactly!" I exclaim. "That's the exact feeling I got from *him*! He talked about her like she was his old lady!"

We all chuckle again until Ronnie lets out a long, deep sigh. "Okay, well, I better get going. Don't go to sleep too late. We have a date at the theatre tomorrow."

"Copy that," I say. Before Ronnie exits the room and shuts the door behind her, I call out her name, and she turns halfway on her heel.

"Yeah?" she inquires from a gap in the doorway.

"What's this thing that Barbara is working on anyways? Her special project?"

Ronnie sighs again. "Don't worry about all that. Get some sleep. She'll explain everything soon enough." And she shuts the door with a thud.

I sink my body onto the bed and adjust my head on the pillow. My eyelids are heavy; I oblige them to close. To say tonight has been a whirlwind of craziness would be an understatement. Cyrinda nuzzles her head against my shoulder again trying to get herself in a sleeping position, but she's so antsy and fidgety that I know she has something to say. She always gets like that when something is on her mind or when she can't sleep.

"What is it?" I practically growl, agitated.

"Nothing, nothing," she responds in typical 'I'm avoiding the question so you can drag it out of me' style.

I shift my hips on the bed. "Don't lie to me. Either tell me what's what or go to sleep. You heard Ronnie. She's being nice enough to take us out tomorrow to try to get jobs. I don't wanna louse this up."

"I know that Trixie, but don't you think we should talk about what happened today? Tonight? Don't you think we should, I don't know? Debrief?" She shimmies her body up closer, so her face is in perfect alignment with mine. Her warm, sweet breath blows hot against my cheek.

"Debrief? What do you mean by that?" I snap.

"I don't know, Trix. All of this … doesn't it feel too … *convenient*?"

"Convenient how? What do you mean?"

"I don't know," she repeats, the timbre of her voice turning desperate and small. "The man who picks us up just happens to know someone along his way? Someone who just so happens to help girls like us?"

"Coincidence," I affirm.

"And this someone who he knows is so *bound* to this strange man that she's willing to take us into her home with no questions asked?"

"Divine intervention," I state with confidence.

"Divine intervention, Trixie? Really? And what about that Sisterhood meeting, and all those candles and the weird ceremony? And what about those bags of blood! You saw all that in the fridge just like I did. What was all *that* about?"

"You heard Ronnie. She said they were from her job."

"Yeah, that's just my point. *Convenient.*"

"Look, I get it," I huff. "I get what you're getting at. I do. Truly. But need I remind you *why* we're here? Do I have to jumpstart your memory about all the shit we left behind?" I try to keep my voice cool and at a low volume, but I can feel it rising with anger.

She shakes her head.

"I was going to kill him. If he hit me one more time, I was going to kill him. And if she had opened up her stupid mouth, I would have killed her too. So, it was either leave when we did or go to jail. 'Cause he certainly wasn't going to stop beating on me, and I certainly wasn't going to let it continue. They called themselves parents?

They were nothing more than monsters collecting a check from the state."

I can feel her hands clench at her side, and she mumbles something inaudible. "I know," she finally whispers.

"So, in my estimation, anywhere is better than there. We're here and now. And what is the here and now?"

"Nowhere."

"Exactly. So, while I can acknowledge that things seem a little off-kilter around here, I'm willing to let all the bizarre little things kinda slide right now because I haven't felt this safe in years. And don't you even try to pretend you don't know what I'm talking about. Now can we please get a little sleep and try to relax?"

"Mmmhmmm," she agrees and twirls strands of my hair around her finger—something she does regularly to help calm her down.

"Goodnight, Cyrinda," I say.

"Your roots are coming in," she deflects.

"I know, Cyrinda. I know."

"Goodnight, Trix," she finally says, and I throw my arm across her.

But I can't sleep. I toss and turn, but only in my head because I'm afraid that if I actually move, I'll wake Cyrinda, and she's resting so peacefully that it'd be a shame to disturb her. She's been through so much, and I know I'm partially to blame for our situation, so I guess I feel like I kinda owe it to her to make sure she's comfortable and safe and taken care of. I guess I've always been protective of her in that respect.

My eyes won't close no matter how hard I try to force them, so I end up staring into the darkness, staring up at the white ceiling. My head spins with everything that transpired the last day, and it almost feels surreal. Like it didn't happen. Like I'm watching a television show or something and I still need to determine if it's a comedy or tragedy. Right now, it feels like a big mystery. Will this be one for *Perry Mason*, or will it end up on *The Alfred Hitchcock Hour?*

A light from the kitchen gently illuminates the hall and creeps its way under the threshold of the bedroom door. Someone's awake, and I can't help but feel even more antsy, even more jittery. Slowly, I pull my arm out from under Cyrinda's head and ease her face onto the thick pillow so her body is unaware of the slight shift. She coos in her sleep, snorts, and brings the blanket up to her chin as she settles back into her dream. I slide off the bed and sneak out the door following the light to the kitchen. As I glide past the dresser, I get a whiff of Ronnie's vial of patchouli oil that sits on a decorative circular mirror, and I almost gag from the smell.

Barbara sits at the circular table with her hands folded pensively. The overhead light makes her pale skin glow with an unnatural radiance, and her eyes light up when I peek my head into the room.

"Trixie? What are you doing awake?" she beams.

"I… I… I couldn't sleep," I answer with a hushed voice.

"Me neither," she huffs and gives me a knowing smile. "Come. Sit. Join me." She motions to the chair next to her.

"Oh, I don't want to bother…"

"Bother me? No! Not a bother at all. Please, sit for a spell. The tea's almost done."

As if on cue, the kettle on the stove whistles its steamy song. "Do you want me to get that?" I ask.

"Would you please? Thank you," she says.

I notice two teacups are already placed at the table, so I bring the hot water over and pour.

Had she been waiting for me? Did she know I was going to get up? That's impossible! I think.

"I know why I'm awake," I say, trying to change the unsettling thoughts in my mind, "but what about you? It's late. What keeps you up?"

Barbara's fingers wrap tightly around the hot cup, and she takes a deep drink. I wince at the thought of the fresh heat directly against my hand and down my throat. *How can she stand that?* She sighs after a long swallow. "Ronnie. In my room with me. She snores." She chuckles, and I give a little giggle in kind. I wasn't expecting that response.

"I'm so sorry if we put you out. We're not going to stay too long, I promise. Then Ronnie can have her room back."

"Absolutely not!" she sings and reaches for my hands. "There's a reason you were brought here to me. We're going to figure that reason out together." She lays her hands over the tops of mine, and I don't know if it's the transfer of heat from her teacup or just her own inner energy, but it feels as if a wave of fire shoots up both my arms. It leaves me feeling all gooey on the inside, like the soft center of a toasted marshmallow. "So, my dear, tell me all about Patricia Bluebell McGovern?"

Instantly, the warm feeling turns to ice. *How did she know my full name? I never told her or Ronnie!*

Barbara's eyes darken, and she pulls her hand away. "Are you okay?" she asks. "Did I say something to upset you?"

"No, no," I brush off, trying to play it cool. *Maybe she overheard Cyrinda call me that?*

"Listen, Trixie, I know this is all weird and new and scary. Anyone in their right mind would be scared half to death if they were in your situation. I just want you to know that I'm here for you. Again, *weird…*" she and I both give a nervous chuckle. "I know what it's like to be lost. To wander. To not have anyone or anything…"

"But I have Cyrinda, so I've been lucky with that," I interject.

"Anyone or anything of concrete substance. A real anchor to keep you grounded. Galen, I mean

Trent, was mine for a little bit, and I trust him with my life and beyond."

"So why aren't you together?"

"It's complicated," she says and there's a deep sadness in her voice. "Maybe one day. Who knows? But we loved to last an eternity, and for that, I am forever bound to him. If he says you are what he says you are, then I wholeheartedly believe him and will obey."

My nose crinkles in confusion. "Says what I am? What did he say I am? When did you speak to him?"

Barbara lets out a bell-like laugh that rings in the space between us and in my head like a musical symphony. "I didn't speak with him, but he has his ways. He touched you, right? Left his mark."

"I'm not sure I understand."

"That's okay," she says and sips the last of her tea.

"What did he say about me?"

Barbara grabs my hand again and holds it in a firm grip. "You are the truth and the light and the way, Trixie."

I don't understand, but something inside me feels happy. At ease. Her words make me feel important and needed, and I can't help but smile dumbly at her as she darts her dark eyes back and forth over mine like she's scanning my brain, searching for something.

"Your mother must be so worried that you ran away," she says sternly. "I know if one of my children left like that, I'd be furious, and worried, and desperate all at the same time."

"You have kids?" I exclaim. I had no idea! There were no signs of children living in the house.

"Something like that," she says, brushing the topic off. "So, your mother…"

"I don't have a mother. Not a real one, at least."

"Ah ha," she says. "That makes sense now."

"What makes sense?"

"And where did you say you were from?" she says, ignoring my inquiry again.

"Indianapolis. My birth parents were in some kind of circus and couldn't keep me, so I was sent to an orphanage and then bounced around from family to family."

"Oh, my dear!" she gasps. "Yes, yes! Perfect sense."

"And that's how Cyrinda and I came to be. So close, I mean. We were both moved from place to place but always together."

"Sister, sister," she hums.

I shrug my shoulders.

"Trixie, I know what it's like. I've gone through something similar, and it's taken me many years to pick up the pieces and right myself. I'm still working on things, ya know? I think that healing is a life-long process. I want to help you heal. I want you to trust me. Because you can trust me. I know I'm still very much a stranger to you, but I promise you this: if you stay with me and help me with what I need, I will make it my business to give you eternal happiness."

Her eyes continue to move side to side, slowly, like a cobra rearing on its tail and sizing up its prey. I fall into them and their hypnotic gaze as a wave of calm rushes over me.

Chapter Five

Friday, April 9th 1965
The Salem Theatre
Corner of S. Broadway and Main Street,
Salem, Illinois
Night of the Half Moon

Just as she had promised, Ronnie took Cyrinda and me to the Salem Theatre the next day to meet with the manager, Julius. And just like she had said, the dude was a complete skuzz. Like totally gross. He looked me up and down with this weird glint in his eye, like I was a piece of meat, and he was hungry. He creeped me out to the max, but I remained poised and polite. I was offered a job, but he all but ignored Cyrinda. When we had gotten home to Barbara's later on she said she wasn't upset—that she didn't want to work in that grody movie theatre anyway. She said she would start looking in the classifieds for something that she was interested in. Ronnie apologized for Julius's inappropriate behavior and promised he was harmless. "He likes to look is all," she had said, and I went along with it because I convinced myself this was only going to be a temporary thing—a super-fast, super-quick, temporary thing. I had to say it like a mantra over and over in order to stomach the entire week's worth of training with him—how he grunted and practically grinded up on me as he showed me how to set the popcorn machine. How he snorted and rubbed his greasy hands over his bulging belly when he showed me how to work the pop machine. How he licked his thick, chapped lips when he showed me how to ring up a customer. I cringed at it all but swallowed my pride and endured.

Super-fast, super-quick, temporary thing.

The movie theatre has four films showing, and thank God Julius put me on concessions because I don't think I'd be able to do the film flippy thing. "Pretty girls front and center, boys in the technical room," he had told me when I asked what my duties were to be. He also told me that I would have a teammate working alongside me, and that took a lot of the pressure off my shoulders.

Ronnie drops me off and waves goodbye as she peels out of the spot in front of the theatre. Barbara allows her to use the car to get back and forth to work, and now part of Ronnie's routine is to get *me* back and forth to *my* work as well.

My work. I breathe in deeply as I enter the low-rent building. The lights inside the lobby are dim—some even flicker every few seconds— and the red carpet is old and worn. Adorning the walls are posters of the movies that are showing currently, but I stop and stare at the "Coming Soon" section: Elvis Presley in *Girl Happy*. I'm not sure why, but I'm drawn to it.

"What a hunk, right?" a female voice says from behind me.

I nod and continue staring. Not because it's Elvis—I don't see Elvis, per se. I see Trent. His face had been fading from my mind since he dropped us off at Barbara's. His mere existence had been slowly disintegrating from my memory the longer time had gone by, but seeing the poster brought me back to that night and how I had initially compared Trent to Elvis.

"I know," the voice says with a giggle. "I'm speechless looking at it, too! I'm so jazzed for that picture to come out next week. Julius said he'll let us come in early to watch it first if we have a good weekend!"

I swivel my head to put a face to the voice, and immediately, I am taken aback. Her face seems vaguely familiar, but I can't place it.

She smiles brightly and puts up two fingers in a peace sign. "June. As in, I am."

It takes a second for her introduction to make sense. I feel like I have to repeat her words in my mind at least three times to come to the conclusion that her name is June. "Trixie," I say, and point stupidly to the plastic name tag on my cranberry blouse.

She smiles again. "Neato! We're partners. Nice to finally meet you, officially, I mean."

My face twists in confusion. "Do I know you?" I ask.

"You're Ronnie's friend. Aren't you staying with Barbara?"

"Uh… yeah…" I stammer, wondering if I should be telling complete strangers my whereabouts.

"Wow!" she gushes. "You really do look like her, don't you?"

"Like who?" I ask, startled.

"Elizabeth Montgomery. She plays Samantha on that show *Bewitched*. Ronnie told Julius you look like her, but much younger, obviously."

"Oh, she said that?"

She moves closer and whispers to me out the side of her mouth like she's telling me the most sacred of secrets. "I've been to some of those Sisterhood meetings over there, ya know." Her eyebrows raise up slowly in perfect rainbow-like arches until the sides of them disappear under her blonde, parted bangs.

Great, I complain to myself, *we have the same hairstyle.* I don't know how to respond to her because I haven't actually *been* to a Sisterhood meeting, but I pretend I know what she's talking about by sweeping my hair behind my ear and nodding intently at her facial expression.

"And that wine that Barbara gives…" Her voice trails as if she's about to say something else, but she stops her initial thought, says, "C'mon," and grabs my hand. She drags me through the lobby and over to the concession stand. "It's almost show time! Friday night is always hopping around here."

Two guys appear from one of the back rooms and sneakily creep over to us at the counter. I jump in surprise as it seems they just poofed up out of thin air. June gasps a "Jesus Christ!" I smirk, thankful I wasn't the only dork who was taken off guard.

"Hey, Junebug!" one of them whispers. He has dark hair and striking, bright blue eyes that reflect the pendant light hanging over the glass counter. "Boss Man around?" He smiles at her, and his face seems to light up the entire area around him. The dim light of the lobby loses its battle against his illuminated grin.

June clicks the roof of her mouth and puts her hand on her hip. "Noooo," she sings. "He's not here yet."

"Far out!" the other exclaims. "Get us some pop before he comes in." He's not as good-looking as his companion, but his cheery voice is almost intoxicating, like I get the sense that he's the life of any party.

She huffs noisily and rolls her eyes, but it's all very playful.

"C'mon, man!" Blue Eyes pleads.

"Fine, fine," she relents, but there's a smirk on her face and a tone in her voice that tells me this is the kind of exchange they have on a regular basis.

June goes to the soda machine and fills two large cups for them. "Here ya go, boys."

"Who's the newbie?" Blue Eyes asks, but he looks directly at me when he says it. His stare burns into my chest, my ears get hot, and I think my cheeks go pink. Thank God the light in here is so low because I'm afraid he'll notice me blushing.

The other with the red curly hair leans over the counter. "Tri-xie," he says reading my name tag.

"Trixie," Blue Eyes repeats, never once breaking his gaze. "I'm Clark."

"And I'm Kent," the other interjects.

I furrow my brow. "Clark and Kent?" I say with disbelief. "You're joking, right?"

The two boys laugh and high-five each other.

"No, unfortunately they are not," June sighs. "And they're not related in any which way. Total coinkydink to add to their utter annoyance."

"Yeah, June, when are you gonna co-ink my dink?" Kent teases.

Again, they go into a round of hysterics and high-fives.

"Har har. You're a funny guy, Kent. Maybe I'll co-ink your dink when you grow up and stop being such a panty waste."

Kent pouts his lower lip and puts a hand over his chest. "You hurt me, Junebug. Deep inside."

The three laugh, and I can't help giggle along with them.

"Yeah, yeah," she says dismissively. "Go back to your dungeons and get those movies playing before Boss Man comes in and catches you screwing around."

"Aye, aye, Captain," Clark says to her, but again I notice, he's looking straight at me.

The two trot off to the back room from where they came.

"Oh, those guys," she says dreamily.

"They run the film?"

"Yep. Cause you know what Julius says."

"Guys in the back, pretty girls in the front?"

"Close enough." She wipes a washrag over the glass countertop erasing the fingerprints the boys left behind.

"You seem to get along with them really well," I say, fishing for some backstory.

"Oh yeah, me and the Supermen go all the way back to grammar school. When you grow up in a small town like Salem, everyone pretty much knows everyone."

"Are you going steady with him?" I inquire.

"With Kent?" she crows. "Good Lord, no!"

"Well, what about Clark?"

"Oh no, not him either. I mean, I think every broad in Salem our age has had a thing for Mr. Clark at one point in time or another, but…" her voice trails as her eyes beam wide open. "Wait a minute! You got a sweet tooth for sweetie?"

I gulp hard. "Well, I mean, he is nice to look at."

She gives me a quick wink. "Okay, okay, new girl. Let me see if I can work my magic!"

I bump my shoulder into hers. "Stop!" I say. "It's not even like that!" And we proceed to giggle.

Suddenly, the doors of the lobby open wide, and patrons begin filtering in with their tickets from the ticket booth in hand. I take a deep breath, and June puts a hand on my shoulder. "Show time," she whispers from the side of her mouth, then turns her attention to the quickly forming line of customers with a big, toothy smile.

Junior Mints, Dots, M&Ms, popcorn… my head spins at each request. Training certainly wasn't as fast-paced as the real-deal, but soon, June and I fall into a steady rhythm of snacks and drinks, snacks, and drinks. I smile as I take their money, smile as I hand them their items, smile as I give them their change. I smile so much I think my face is going to fall off.

"This is your first job, isn't it?" she whispers to me between customers.

I nod and keep moving. Keep moving. Keep serving. Keep smiling.

I'm in such a state of constant motion that I scarcely notice I have served the same towheaded boy at least three times already tonight. When he approaches the counter for the fourth time and asks for more popcorn, I stop dead in my tracks and do a double-take. "You've been here all night, haven't you!" I exclaim.

He lowers his head sheepishly and nods. "Yeah," he says, "I like movies. What can I say?"

"So, what did you see?"

"*Tom and Jerry* was first. Then I saw *My Fair Lady*. Now I'm going in to see *The Holy Terror*." He's nervous. Fidgety. But his face suddenly lights up when he starts talking about the films as if no one has ever asked him about his love of the theatre before.

"By yourself?"

He nods. "I like to watch by myself. People distract me."

"Well, maybe you're not watching with the *right* people," I say handing him his popcorn.

He looks up at me from his shaggy bangs, his blond wannabe Beatles haircut, and smiles. But it's a cold and vacant one that kinda creeps me out. Like he's here in front of me, but not really. I hadn't noticed it until I engaged him in conversation, but my insides scream at me to walk away— to get away from this stiff.

"Maybe you can watch movies with me?" he says in a low tone, and the hairs on my arms stand straight up. There's a strange vacancy in his eyes that I find peculiar and unnerving.

Having heard the entire exchange, June races over to my side and pulls me at the elbow. "Oh, now, now," she sings with a pleasant tune. "We're not allowed to fraternize with the customers. Come with me, Trixie, and help me with the soda fountain? I think something is stuck inside it."

"Yeah, yeah, sure," I mumble as I hand the weird guy his change. "Excuse me, I have to…" I say to him.

He puts up his hand and waves me on to follow behind June.

"Enjoy your show!" I call out over my shoulder as I make my way to the soda machine.

June tugs down hard on my arm. "What the hell were you doing?" she chastises.

Flabbergasted, I am at a loss for words.

"Trixie! You can't be all *flirty-flirty* with the customers."

"I... I wasn't... I... I didn't..." I stammer, confused.

"Coulda fooled me! You were giving off the energy that you were gonna jump his bones or something."

"What? No! Definitely not!"

"Look, I get it. You're a total dish, but just don't be overly friendly with the customers. Especially *that* one."

Now I'm supremely confused. Why did June say that I'm pretty? I'm not pretty! No way! Either she's just trying to make me feel good, or she's totally fibbing. Or both. I mean, I know I'm not like a total dog or anything, but I would never look in the mirror and think to myself that I was a "total dish" like June said. I would classify June as pretty. Model pretty. Cover of *Vogue* pretty. Ok, maybe not cover, but definitely a fashion spread on the inside. Barbara is cover material. No. That's not right. Barbara is something else. Barbara isn't model pretty, she's beyond that. Barbara sparkles. Barbara glows. Barbara floats when she walks through the house, and the space around her glimmers and shimmers with her every move. Like how the library in the den of her house twinkles at me in the candlelight. Like how…

"That's Carny John. He's here every weekend," June's voice snaps me back into focus.

"Carny John?" I ask, dazed. "Why do you call him Carny John?"

"No idea. We just do. I think someone once said his family is a bunch of circus freaks or something."

I go cold, like I freeze for a second. I know the circus all too well… "He kinda looks like a circus freak," I mumble, trying to cover up any weird expression my face possibly revealed.

"Trixie! That's not the point. Carny John is here every weekend, and he's always by himself. Always. He's creepy, but pretty much harmless. You just can't engage him cause he has a tendency to get all weird and shit. He was weird with the girl who had your spot a few months back."

"Weird how?"

She shrugs her shoulders. "I dunno. Just weird. Crazy eyes and always looming around. Saying weird shit. Inappropriate shit. Kent swears Carny John jacks off in the men's room, and Clark says he's seen him going through the dumpsters."

I stick out my tongue and knit my eyebrows. "Ewwww! That's disgusting!"

June snorts. "Yeah, which part?"

"All of it! So nasty!"

"Promise me you keep your dealings with him to food and money only!"

I nod fervently, and we both walk back to the counter.

Later on, we watch as the movie-goers file out of the theatre, and we straighten up for the night. Clark and Kent meet us at the counter, and when Julius does his final walk-through to make sure everything is spic and span, we all walk out to the parking lot in the back where their car is parked. Apparently, they all ride together in Clark's car.

"You need a ride, Trixie?" June asks.

"Oh, no thank you. I'm waiting to get picked up."

Clark and Kent slow down to see if I'm going to be joining them.

"Well, we'll wait with you," Clark says. "It's late. You shouldn't be out here alone."

I hitchhiked here from Indianapolis! If that didn't kill me, I don't think standing alone in the dark for a few minutes will. "I'll be fine. Ronnie won't be much longer."

But Clark and June give each other a sideways glance that makes me nervous. "No, no," June insists. "We can wait with you. Strength in numbers."

I huff loudly. "I promise, I'm fine."

"No, Trixie, really," Kent says. "People sorta have a tendency to go missing in this town."

June swats his shoulder. "Kent! Don't scare her!"

"What do you mean, 'go missing?'" I ask slowly. There's about a cup of curiosity mixed with a dash of fear in my voice.

"Girls. Teenagers—like you and June. Just kinda sorta… I don't know… *vanish*," Clark adds in a low voice.

My face twists, and I run my fingers nervously through my hair. *Probably just runaways. Like me.*

Somebody somewhere back in Indianapolis is probably saying the same thing about me and Cyrinda right about now. Maybe my social worker, or maybe my foster parents (but I doubt it). Maybe one of my teachers is lamenting over the loss of my superior skills in their class. Yeah, right. I bet they don't even give a shit that I'm gone.

"How well do you know Ronnie, anyway?" June asks.

Her question takes me off guard, and before I get a chance to answer, Barbara's Ford vrooms into the parking lot with Ronnie laying a heavy hand on the horn.

"See, told ya she'd be here lickety-split!" I say with a smile.

"Okay," Clark says.

"See ya tomorrow, Trixie," June says with a wave, but her voice is small and concerning.

Kent gives me a head nod, and they hop into Clark's car. I watch them intently as I open the passenger side door, but something from the corner of my eye catches my attention, and I swivel my head to look back toward the side of the building before I get in. Something seems to move behind the green dumpsters. At first, I think it's Julius taking out the garbage, but the longer I stare, the more I realize someone's there—hanging out there, standing there, hiding out there, *watching us* from there.

"Trixie?" Ronnie says. "You okay? You gettin' in?"

"Yeah, yeah," I mutter, but I don't take my eyes off the area by the back door of the theatre as I slip into the front seat.

"How was your first real day?" Ronnie asks happily, like how a mom would ask their child about their first day of school.

"Great," I respond. "I like the people I work with, so that's a bonus."

"Neato," Ronnie replies, and she makes a U-turn and exits the parking lot.

As she turns around the bend, I look into the rearview mirror, my eyes fixated on the dumpsters. And there, to my surprise, Carny John weasels his way out from behind the green canister and goes trotting off down Main Street.

Chapter Six

Friday, April 9th 1965
Barbara Thorne's House
163 North Shelby Avenue
Salem, Illinois
Night of the Half Moon

My eyes open wide as I'm jarred out of a dreamless sleep. There's that weird state of confusion upon waking—*Where am I? Who am I? Am I still dreaming?* It takes me a few seconds to get my bearings as the events of the last twenty-four hours click to life in my brain. Cyrinda is still fast asleep beside me. In her violent slumber, she's curled herself up in the fetal position with her back to me. So, I lie there, soaking in the unfamiliar atmosphere of the room and the bed, and I try tuning my ears into the unfamiliar sounds the old house makes alongside the soft cacophony of the nighttime insects singing their song outside. My brain searches for the sound that had woken me up, but there's nothing out of the ordinary. In the quiet, hushed moments I think that maybe it's just my nerves that jolted me awake, but then

I hear something indistinct from the next room. A muffling sound. A shuffling sound. A growing, muted noise that swells into voices talking, voices talking, voices…

Moaning.

It's low, and deep, and I get the sense that whoever makes the noise is trying hard to conceal it but, for whatever reason, can't. Like, there's a palpable struggle behind the wall.

It's a woman with the voice of a bell. Barbara, I surmise. I can't remember if she told us she had a boyfriend or not, but by the sounds coming from her room, there's no denying she has "company."

I shake Cyrinda's shoulder. "Cyri!" I whisper excitedly, but she doesn't move. She's dead to the world, so I don't press the issue. Instead, I slink off my side of the bed and crawl over to the door to get a better listen. Immediately, I recognize it as someone in the heat of the moment, and I giggle a little at the prospect of witnessing Barbara in the throes of passion.

The moans get louder, more fever-like, more uncontrolled. It's a sound that comes from deep down in the chest, rises with passion to the throat, and hums against the roof of the mouth. It's a sound that longs to be set free with wild abandon but is stifled by the biting of the lower lip. I don't know from experience, but friends talk. People talk. And foster parents don't give a shit about what the kids hear. I can't deny my curiosity as a twitching sensation in my stomach brings a gush of excitement to my panties, so cautiously I creak open my door. I stay low to the ground and pray to God I'm well-concealed.

Barbara's bedroom door is wide open, and the soft glimmer of candlelight radiates throughout the room and spills out into the hallway, and I am thankful to be just outside the glow of it.

That can't be! I think to myself as I spy from my crouched position.

But it is. And my mind has trouble processing the images. For a moment I think I must be still dreaming because everything is white and hazy like a fog has blanketed the entire home. I watch what's happening in there as if I was watching a movie. It feels like time has slowed down, and there's a faint, muffled sound of music in the background like someone's got a record player on somewhere.

Barbara's naked body is spread eagle on her bed. She is firm and soft at the same time, and she clutches her heavy breasts with one hand as her nails make indents in her white, porcelain-like skin. Curiously, in her other hand is an ornate hand-held mirror. Judging from the intricate design, it must be an antique. She holds it up and out so she can see herself—watch herself—touching her bosom and rolling her nipple between her two fingers. She squirms as she touches herself, and I squint a little to get a better view.

'Cause I am in awe. Paralyzed with curiosity.

Barbara bends her legs at the knees as another naked figure appears from the other corner of the room. Quickly I recognize Ronnie with her tall and slender body and cropped black hair. She's wearing rubber gloves. Surgical gloves. And she's carrying one of the blood bags from the fridge!

No, this isn't right. This isn't possible. I'm still dreaming. Trixie, wake up!

I squint harder and inch my body out into the hallway a little more but am careful not to step into the light from Barbara's room.

Ronnie kneels on the edge of the bed in between Barbara's legs and presses a thumb into Barbara's nether region. She massages her outer lips with a roundhouse motion as Barbara moans in delight again. She adjusts the mirror higher above her head and bites her lower lip like she's taking seductive pictures for some nudey magazine. "Yes!" she says breathlessly, and Ronnie rubs her harder and deeper. I can't tell if her thumb is actually penetrating Barbara's sex, but by the way Barbara responds, Ronnie's finger is definitely in the outer pleasure zone.

I squint some more because something shifts in the room. Something is off, and I can't decipher what happened. It looks like how a TV looks when you turn it on and the picture kind of crackles to life. That's what happened in the room. A crackle. A static-y ripple. Barbara tilts the mirror above her, and a thin line of light reflects onto the ceiling. But there's no above-head light to shine onto the mirror's face! And suddenly, a hole opens up in the ceiling and the light of a thousand stars twinkles into the room.

How can this be? How can this be? This is a dream!

"Yes! Now!" Barbara commands, and Ronnie stops to open one of the valves of the blood bag. She spills the dark red liquid onto Barbara's stomach making the shape of a star in a circle. *A pentagram?* The blood looks black against Barbara's pale skin, and the shape of the star drips down the sides of her torso and onto the yellow comforter on the bed. "Now!" Barbara repeats as she continues watching herself in the mirror. Ronnie coats two fingers on her right hand in the blood, then opens Barbara's legs wider, and jams them inside of her.

Barbara's body jolts from the initial insertion, and she gasps with delight. Ronnie presses into her—back and forth, deep, and slow, then shallow and quick. Barbara rides with Ronnie's fingers. She bucks her hips up and down, tilts the mirror back down, and admires herself again as Ronnie relentlessly fingers her. She smiles in the mirror—smiles and bites her lower lip, and I get the odd feeling that she sees something other than her reflection.

I feel dizzy. Sleepy. My mind isn't processing properly, as I repeat to myself this is all a dream… all a dream… all a…

"Just like that," Barbara moans to Ronnie and into the mirror. "Not much longer." And her breathing becomes more of a pant. I can tell she's on the verge of orgasm. Ronnie senses it too as she quickens the pace, assaulting Barbara's private area with frenzied motions. I think the music gets louder from that faraway place. *Maybe they have a Victrola in the closest?* But it's not any song or kind of music I've ever heard before. It sounds weird. Like people playing random instruments and singing out of tune all together and all at once. It hurts my ears when it gets louder. I try to understand the words, try to pinpoint the types of instruments, but I can't. It's too bizarre to distinguish what the sounds actually are. At one point, I think I hear a growl and a baby crying.

Barbara lets out another passionate "Yes," and Ronnie quickly removes her fingers and inserts the tip of the blood bag inside her. With a final squeeze, she shoots what's left of the blood inside as Barbara squeals with satisfied delight. Her body relaxes, and Ronnie climbs on top of her for an embrace. The sticky blood smears between their two heated bodies. The music stops, and the hole in the ceiling instantly closes.

I shudder. I close my eyes for a second as I wince, but the bizarre images are burned so deep.

This is all a dream. This is all a dream. This is all a... But like a car crash, I am compelled to look, compelled to observe the horrors before me.

Barbara puts the mirror on the nightstand next to her bed, wraps her arms around Ronnie's back, and kisses the top of her head.

Horrified, I begin to slowly creep backward into my room. I pray every inch of the way that they won't hear me. I pray every step I take they are so distracted by their weirdo sex ritual that...

This is all a dream. This is all a dream. This is all a...

"Trixie," a voice whispers, and I assume it's Cyrinda, but when I get my body fully into the room and gently close the door, she's still in the same fetal position I left her in.

A chill races up my spine, and I trot over to the bed and jump under the covers.

"Trixie," the whisper says again, only this time louder in my head. "It's okay to watch."

Mortified and confused, I throw the blanket over my head.

But the area between my legs kinda throbs.

The images of what I witnessed flash in my mind even though I try desperately to shut them out, and before I even realize it, or try to stop myself, my hand moves down the front of my body, snakes under the top of my panties, and gently kneads my lady parts until I fall asleep, because even though I've never known a man in a sexual way in my entire life thus far, I'm certainly no stranger to my own fingers.

Sunday, April 18th 1965
Afternoon of the Waning Gibbous Moon

I work as much as I could at the theatre, and really enjoy being with June and the guys. The three of them are super nice, and we all get along so well. I've been a little leery about telling them too much about myself, but I know with time, that'll fade away. June says I fit right in. That makes me happy. I've never felt like I fit in any-where my entire life—except when I am with Cyrinda. See, when I was two, my birth parents put me up for adoption. I was in an orphanage for a flash of a second and then the place burned to the ground. The kids who survived all got split up into various foster homes, and that's where Cyrinda and I crossed paths for the first time. The two of us were given to the same family, and that began our adventures in foster home hopping.

Along with a long laundry list of atrocities that came with it.

Besides, my movie theatre gig is a major dis-traction from the pink elephant in the room. I have felt like I had to walk on eggshells since witnessing what happened in Barbara's room. Neither Ronnie nor Barbara have mentioned anything to me, and I haven't said a gosh-darn word, but heck, I get this feeling that they know I know. I get this feeling that they know I know they know. So, I'm stuck in this weird circle of shame and anxiety. I'm not even sure if what I saw actually happened, because when I think about it—when I think long and hard and try to reimagine the images clearly in my mind—it all seems fuzzy and hazy like a drunken dream. I doubt my memory so much, that I don't even tell Cyrinda what I saw. She either wouldn't believe it or would insist we leave Barbara's house immediately.

And I'm kinda not ready to do that just yet.

I told Cyrinda about the movie crew, and when Julius allowed us to have a private screening of the new Elvis movie before it hit theatres (like June said he would), I dragged her along. Clark picked us up, and we went out for burgers and shakes before heading to the movie house. To be honest, *Girl Happy* wasn't great, but it's always a treat seeing Elvis on the big screen, and the movie crew is so much fun to be around that I pretty much laughed all night. Cyrinda was her usual, shy-as-a-church-mouse-self, which didn't surprise me at all. She barely joined the conversations and kept to herself a lot. When we got back home to Barbara's that night, Cyrinda complained how she felt uncomfortable and out of place, quite the opposite to how I felt. She said she felt ignored by the others like she didn't exist or something. I told her that she was being paranoid and overly dramatic and that it was all in her head. I told her they liked her a lot (even though I hadn't confirmed as much with June) and that she needed to be less standoffish the next time we all hung out.

"There's not gonna be a next time, Trix," she had barked at me. "Those are your friends, not mine."

I didn't press the issue further because that same night she said she wasn't feeling very well. At first, I thought she was faking it and was trying to get out of hitting the pavement for a job, but I was so wrong! Cyrinda has been in bed for a few days now, and I'm a little worried about what it could be.

I hope it's not the flu. I hate the goddamn flu! This one time I had the flu when I was eight years old. My foster mom didn't believe me when I told her I wasn't feeling well. She didn't take my temperature or even touch me to feel if I was warm. My fever spiked so high that that night I started hallucinating. At first, the pretty flowers on my wallpaper started to dance around in the air. The petals came right off the stems and blew gently in the breeze and all around me. Oh, I had laughed and laughed! I think my foster father yelled from the other room, "Quit yer laughin'," but I can't remember. The petals had sung songs—beautiful music filled my head like I was at a grand symphony. But when the petals fell onto my bed, they changed shape, melded together, and a dark and twisted creature with the body of a dandelion and the face of a gargoyle rose up. He snarled and reached for me with his boney, furry hand. I panicked, and started to scream, "Don't get me! Don't get me!" The screaming continued until I lost my breath, passed out, and fell off the bed onto the hardwood floor. My foster mother came bounding into my room when she heard the *thud*. She swooped me off the floor, and later she told me I was so hot with fever, it felt like I would burn right through her clothes.

Whenever Cyrinda or I aren't feeling well, the other makes some chicken lentil soup, so I figure I will whip some up for her before I head out to work. I know I am daydreaming as I mindlessly stirred the soup counterclockwise in the pot, but I guess I didn't realize for exactly how long I had been in 'la-la' land. Before I knew it, Barbara was standing in the kitchen doorway with her hand on her hip, practically screaming my name. "Trixie! Trixie! What on earth are you doing? Ronnie is waiting to take you to work!"

I blink my eyes rapidly as her perfect form comes into my vision. For a fraction of a moment, seeing her face and hearing her voice sets my soul at ease, and all my worrying about Cyrinda seems to melt away like the last snowfall of winter waking up to spring's embrace.

"Oh," I say, startled, taken off guard. "I'm just gonna bring this to…" I jut my chin out toward the hallway where Cyrinda and my room is. "I'll be right there." Barbara's left eye does a weird twitchy thing, and her shoulders slowly relax. I fear that I've maybe offended her in some way, so I increase the urgency in my step and quickly ladle the soup into a bowl.

Barbara stops me before I can turn down the hallway and places her hands on my shoulders. "You're a good person," she says, but I find it odd that I don't see her lips move when she speaks. Regardless, her voice fills my head with a feeling of pure euphoria. I feel as light as a feather—like I am walking on cloud nine just being in close proximity to her. "You should be proud of yourself for how far you've come," she seems to sing, but the words don't really sound like words anymore—it's more of a song. No. Music. Like the music I heard the night Barbara and Ronnie were drenched in blood on Barbara's bed with the yellow sheets. Then I realize, Barbara doesn't have yellow sheets! They're white with little pink flowers all over them. I saw them the other day when I was helping with the laundry. I try to dig in my brain to recall the images I saw that night— that night with the blood, and the mirror, and the music, and the candles, and…

Barbara lets out a little chuckle, and suddenly I feel confused and a little bit ashamed for thinking those vulgar and horrific things that *clearly* didn't happen.

Or did they? I don't know, I can't be sure anymore…

"The people you work with," she says. "Are they nice? They treating you well?"

"Oh absolutely," I say, bobbing my head up and down. "Super nice. They make the time go by so much faster."

"That's good. Now hurry. Don't keep Ronnie waiting too long."

I nod and scurry by her in the doorway but stop and do a quick turn on my heel. "Hey, Barbara, ya know the girl I work with, June? She's been here at some of your Sisterhood meetings." I smile, like I know something grand and wonderful. Like I'm making a connection with Barbara on a more personal level, but she shifts her weight to one side and flings her long brown hair over her shoulder.

"Is that right?" she says.

"Yeah. She's a cute little blonde. Same haircut as me."

"And she was here the night you showed up?"

"Mmmhmmm," I say and nod again.

"Well, when we have our meeting next month, be sure to tell her to come back. We're all sisters in the circle." She smiles with her lips closed tightly together, and her eye does that little open-closey thing again.

"Groovy. I will," I say and make my way to the bedroom.

Cyrinda is out cold when I creak the door open, so I leave the bowl of soup next to the night-stand. Gently, I lean forward to feel her forehead to see if she has a fever or not, but I'm stopped in my tracks by the loud blare of the car horn, and Ronnie's muffled voice from behind the driver's seat screaming my name. I tip-toe out and shut the door behind me.

Chapter Seven

Sunday, April 18th 1965
The Salem Theatre
Corner of S. Broadway and Main Street, Salem, Illinois
Night of the Waning Gibbous Moon

The theatre is definitely buzzing with electric energy tonight! The line to the ticket booth is down to the corner of the block, and Julius already has the popcorn machine fired up and ready to go.

"Brace yourself, ladies," he says to June and me. "This is Elvis night."

"You know, Jules," she says with a lazy lilt in her voice. "That movie wasn't that great."

"You know, June," he repeats her cadence in a sarcastic way, "that's something best kept to yourself."

June and I laugh as the boss man stalks away.

"The guys here?" I ask.

"Yep. Got here extra early 'cause you-know-who wanted everything to be in tip-top."

"For sure."

"After work tonight, me and the boys are gonna go out to the Shake Shack for some burgers. Wanna come?"

I run my hands up and down my uniform. *Yes! Yes, I would very much enjoy that!* I want to scream, but the thought of Cyrinda being sick in bed makes me hold my tongue and hesitate. "I... I don't think so. Not tonight. Ronnie's picking me up and..."

"We'll take you home. It's no problem," she tries coaxing me.

"It's just that I have no way of telling Ronnie not to come out here to pick me up. Like, maybe next time I can let her know beforehand and..."

"You trust her?" she asks, cutting me off, and I'm taken aback by the abruptness of her question.

"Huh? What do you mean? That's kind of a weird question. I don't know if I like, *trust* her trust her, but she and Barbara have been good to us, so..."

June clicks her tongue against the roof of her mouth and doesn't respond.

"What? What's that look for?" I press.

"I don't know," she says hesitantly. "Ronnie was like a real good friend of this girl I know. We all hung out in the same circle, but I was never close or anything to her. Anyway, Barbara just like kinda showed up in town one day, and Ronnie just kinda cut everyone out to be with her."

Which I totally understand...

"And then the whole Sisterhood thing. A lot of us girls would go every now and then to these meetings. Don't get me wrong. They're great and all. Barbara tells good stories and knows how to make you feel really good about yourself. It's really nice to bond with other girls and get some of the brain junk out."

"I've only walked in on the end of the last one. The one you were at a few weeks ago. Barbara actually told me to tell you not to forget the next one next month."

June's face goes white.

"What's wrong? Are you okay?"

"Yeah, about that…" her voice trails. "I don't know if I'm gonna go."

"Why? How come? You said it was good to do the whole female bonding thing."

"I don't know, Trixie. It just felt… *off*? I don't think I'm explaining it right."

"Well, try. Tell me. What felt off?"

She leans in closer to me and lowers both her head and her voice. "I don't know about all the witch stuff. Ronnie told me that the Sisterhood is like the first level or something, but then the deeper you get in with them they're like a coven or something."

"A coven?"

"I don't know," she kinda stammers. "A red coven, or a crimson coven? Something with a color. At first, it was fun and cool and all power-to-the-sister, but…"

I shrug my shoulders.

"Have you ever heard of the word *Blodheksa*?"

"Blood-what?" I say, my voice markedly louder than hers.

"Shhh," she admonishes, "lower your voice. Blodheksa," she repeats.

"No," I say, shaking my head. "I've never heard of that word. What does it mean?"

Nervously, she tucks her blonde hair behind her ear, and I notice a small gold hoop earring dangling from her earlobe. *Expensive,* I think. *Probably her Sweet 16 gift or something.* She leans in closer to me. "It means Blood Witch," she says.

"What in the hell is a Blood Witch?" I crow.

June shuffles in place, the hesitation and fear ooze from her stance. But just as she's about to open her mouth to speak, Julius opens the lobby doors with a bellowing "Showtime!" and a horde of movie-goers descends upon us.

The chaos begins as the customers crowd the counter eager to get their snacks and drinks, hoping to be the first in the theatre for the best seat in the house. It's a non-stop wave of food and money (and all that smiling again). At one point, June drops a soda down the front of her shirt leaving a large, wet stain right on her chest. It only draws more attention to their voluptuousness, but she powers through it and remains poised and calm. *That's skill,* I think.

Carny John makes his usual one, two, three appearances throughout the night. His white greasy hair hangs low over his eyes and sticks to the skin of his forehead. He smirks at me when I serve him, but I make sure not to say much more than "Thank you" and "Here you go." When I say, "Enjoy the show" on his third time to the stand, he mumbles something back to me. I know I should have ignored it, but I instinctually question him. "Huh?"

"I said, I was wondering if you wanted to enjoy the show," he says as he stares directly into my eyes.

It weirds me out so much that I quickly glance away. "You know the rules," I say to the countertop, but trying to maintain a friendly tone.

"What about when you're not working?" he presses.

"I can't," I say nervously. "I have a boyfriend."

Carny John stiffens, and his eyes darken something awful. "Oh," he says curtly. "Is it one of those guys who work here?"

I don't like the tone of his voice. It makes the hair on the back of my neck stand up, and a static-y noise rises in my ears like some kind of warning bell. June is too preoccupied with another customer to step in and save the day, so I think fast, slide his box of M&M's over to him, and feign a laugh. "Oh you! You better get to your seat, or you'll miss the opening scene!"

He snatches his candy off the counter and storms away, and I exhale loudly with a sigh of relief.

Later that night, we clean up and lock up like usual, and the four of us head out to the parking lot. It's a chilly night; June doesn't have her sweater, and after being doused with a large cup of pop, she's got some shivers happening on her lips. I feel bad making her stand there waiting for me to get picked up, so I tell them all to leave. "Ronnie's never been late. She'll be here soon. I'll be fine."

She looks at me with half concern and half relief. "Are you sure? Are you absolutely positive?" she asks.

"Of course," I say, waving my hands in the air. "She's probably less than ten minutes away."

"Are you sure you don't wanna come hang with us?" she asks again.

"Positive. We'll hang out next time."

"Promise?"

"I promise," I say and make a cross gesture with my pointer finger over my chest. "Cross my heart."

June nods to the boys and they wave their goodbyes and walk over to their car. "See ya," she sings and disappears into the backseat.

I wrap my arms around my shoulders and breathe out. My breath is a smoky white puff of air, and for a split second, I pretend it's cigarette smoke that I exhale. Putting my two fingers up to my mouth, I pretend to take a long, deep drag on a cancer stick and try to make 'O' rings with the smoke.

I'm such a badass, smoking on a cig late at night ... by myself ... in a parking lot. Such a tough girl. Wild child.

I giggle out loud at my ridiculous thoughts when I hear something rustle over by the dumpsters.

Must be a rat. I think.

But it happens again, and a shiver runs through me. Suddenly, my "aloneness" doesn't feel so alone, and my insides don't feel like much of a badass. In fact, they feel like a gelatinous pile of gloppy goo, and I can't figure out why. I swallow hard, trying to push the sensation of nausea back down my throat, but it doesn't seem to work. I feel like I'm going to barf.

Again, a noise, and my limbs go rigid. "Hello?" I call out, like an idiot, because if it is a just a rat, then a response is definitely not coming. And if it isn't a rat? Why the hell did I just invite a response that I know I don't want to hear?

Ronnie needs to get here soon.

The lot isn't that big but standing here feeling as small and as alone as I do right now, makes the area around me feel like it's an open expanse of infinity.

You're not alone, a voice says, and I jerk my body around wildly to see where it came from.

"Who's there?" I call out nervously.

More rustling from the dumpsters, and before I know it, a masked figure dressed in black rushes out from behind the bins and is on me in a matter of seconds.

I have no time to move, no time to scream, no time to even breathe. The assailant knocks me down and sits on top of my waist, pinning me to the ground. I squirm and squeal and try to flail around enough in hopes of getting away, but I'm too stunned, too shocked, and above all—too weak to fight out of his hold. "Stop! Don't!" I manage to scream as he claws at my blouse. I know it's a "he" by the sheer weight and force and roughness of his actions.

"Shut up!" he growls and stares at me with his empty eyes.

Instantly, I recognize the voice, I recognize the weird gaze. "Carny John?" I cry out.

He grabs my shoulders and slams my upper body against the pavement. "Shut up!" he repeats. "Shut up and be fucking still!"

My mind goes blank, and I kind of detach myself from myself—both mentally and spiritually—because I know what Carny John intends to do, and I am so frozen with fear that I am powerless to stop it from happening.

"You don't have to do this!" I cry, hot tears flowing down my cheeks.

That enrages him and he tears my shirt down from the top. Every button pops loose, and I hear their tiny *pingings* of plastic as they bounce on the concrete next to my ears. "I said to shut the fuck up! Why are you making me do this?"

He takes one of my breasts in his hand and squeezes down hard. I wiggle against him, but his legs tighten around my waist like a vice.

"I'm not! I'm not! Please stop!" I beg.

Please Ronnie. Please Ronnie. Please Ronnie.

As if my prayers had been answered, the headlights of Barbara's car come shining into the parking lot. Like an angel from a gasoline-filled heaven, the engine roars as it speeds up and swerves dangerously close to me on the ground. Startled, Carny John rolls off me and out of the way, but the car circles around, boxing him in. I scramble to my feet and hurry over when the car stops.

Barbara gets out of the passenger side and motions for me to get in. Slowly, she saunters over to Carny John who stands still in the middle of the lot. His eyes are wide with fear, and I wonder why he doesn't just run away.

Just run away, John. Just run…

And that's when I realize he most certainly *wants* to run away. He just *can't*. I think he's paralyzed. He physically cannot move.

"What's going on?" I say frantically to Ronnie when I get in the car.

"Don't worry," she says calmly. "Are you okay?"

I nod my head, but it throbs so fiercely that my vision starts to thump in time with it.

"Did he…"

"No. No. But he tried."

The scent of something burning hits the air, and Carny John lets out a horrific scream. I train my eyes on what's happening, but everything is blurry—my shock and my tears and the raging thumping in my head give the world a crazy, jagged look.

"Your head is bleeding," Ronnie remarks calmly. I look down at my collar, and sure enough, my blood has decorated the edges. She leans over me, opens the glovebox, and hands me a handkerchief. "Hold that against it."

I bring the cloth to the back of my head and press hard to try to stop the bleeding. My head must have split open when Carny John rushed me to the ground, but for some reason, I don't really care about that. My focus is zoned in to what's happening in the lot between Barbara and my attacker. "What is she saying to him? What is she doing to him?" I ask, and my voice sounds far away, like from another time and space.

"What she needs to," Ronnie responds nonchalantly.

"But he's..."

Carny John howls. Yelps. Falls to his knees in agonizing pain, yet Barbara is but three or four feet away from him. She has no weapons. She's not even within striking distance to kick him in the nuts! "Ronnie!" I exclaim. "How can she—? What is she—?"

Again, he moans with a deep, bellowing tone, and for some reason, I feel like that's what it must sound like to be a soul in Hell—the agony in the sound, the torment in the sound, the everlasting and unstoppable pain in the sound—until he curls up in the fetal position and rocks back and forth.

Barbara comes back to the car and hops into the back seat. She puts one hand on my shoulders and the other on the back of my head at the laceration. "It's okay now." Her hands are hot, like she has just pulled them from a blazing inferno. The heat radiates throughout my body, and I feel like I might burn on the inside. The hand at my head is scalding—a searing pain jolts through my skull like a hot poker cauterizing an open wound in Medieval times. "You're safe now," she whispers.

But her voice is not a voice. The words come out like the popping noises from a forest fire.

Chapter Eight

Friday, April 23rd 1965
The Salem Theatre
Corner of S. Broadway and Main Street,
Salem, Illinois
Night of the Half Moon

When I had gotten home the night Barbara scared Carny John away, I was on cloud nine. Maybe it was a rush of adrenaline, maybe it was a side effect from my head injury, maybe it was my flight or fight inside response, who knows for sure. But I felt cloudy and fuzzy, and invincible all at the same time. I profusely thanked Ronnie and Barbara for coming to my rescue right in the nick of time and told them how I couldn't understand how June could ever doubt their noble intentions. When I walked into my room to tell Cyrinda, I was immediately put off when I saw she hadn't touched the soup I had made her. She didn't seem too impressed with the situation either. As a matter of fact, she seemed very upset by it, and not by the fact that Carny John ripped off my shirt and pinned me to the ground. As I relayed the story of my almost rape, she pouted, sighed, and said, "Patricia Bluebell McGovern" with such sadness and bewilderment in her voice that it threw me into such a tizzy. She knows how much I hate it when she calls me by my full name, so I pouted and fussed right back at her.

It's no secret that she and I haven't quite been seeing eye to eye since we got here. And while I want to feel empathetic to her not being well, she's making it very hard for me to give her the benefit of the doubt.

Cyrinda stayed in bed all week again, and of course I've been taking care of her. I certainly can't ask Barbara or Ronnie to help. Ronnie works every day at the blood bank, and Barbara… well, I think Barbara has a job, but I'm not quite sure what she does all day long. Sometimes my time here during the week is hazy and jumbled, but Barbara leaves at some point each day and I assume it's to go to work. Or something. I… I don't really know. I don't even think it's that important. I'm just so grateful that she is allowing us to stay, so I can't ask questions and I can't ask for help with Cyrinda. Cyrinda is my responsibility. We're a package deal. *Me and my shadow.* And at the end of the day, I truly don't mind because, if not for Cyrinda, Lord only knows where I'd be. She's saved me so many times, I can't even begin to count, so taking care of flu-baby Cyri is the least I could do. Although, I'd be lying if I said I wasn't deathly afraid of catching whatever she has, so I've slept out on the couch in the living room for the last week.

When I walk into the movie theatre to start my shift, there's a weird kind of silence that blankets the air. A part of me breathes the air of relaxation knowing Carny John is not coming back. Definitely not. I know in my heart I will never see him ever again. Barbara saw to that. I don't know what she said, or what she did, but I know that he will be forever tormented by that night. Actually, I wouldn't be surprised if he went home and committed suicide! And how would I know? I guess the only part of me that cares is my curiosity, so…

Suddenly I realize I'm alone. My senses pick up on people milling about in the back rooms, and I suspect it's Clark and Kent, but there's no permeating dominant presence of Julius, and as I look around myself and throughout the lobby, I realize, there's no June.

She probably got the flu too, which means I'm gonna be next. Great. Just what I goddamn need. The flu. Shit!

I throw my hands up in defeat and get straight to work. If June is sick, there's nothing I can do about it except get through the night by myself. I was fully aware this was bound to happen sometime, so I kick it into high gear and brace myself for a busy night. Thank God there aren't any major releases this weekend—just the Elvis leftovers and repeats from the previous weeks.

Voices from the anteroom get louder, and the lobby door opens swiftly. I'm taken off guard because I still have about fifteen minutes before patrons filter in, so I stop wiping down the glass countertop and look up. Julius holds the door for an older woman, and as he ushers her in, he mumbles something and points over in my direction. The woman darts around his big gut and trots over to me at the concession stand as I freeze on the inside. As she approaches, I notice her blonde hair is frazzled and unkempt, and her face is long and weary like she'd been crying for a thousand forevers. There is something oddly familiar in her facial features and mannerisms that make me do a total double take.

The woman holds a stack of papers against her chest, and my insides go numb.

They found me, I think. *She's some kind of private investigator sent to pick me up and haul me back to Indianapolis.*

I steel myself and wring my hands together when she demands, "Are you Trixie?" She eyes me up and down and focuses on the name tag on my shirt, and I can't help but mentally smack myself in the face for not giving everyone a fake name. I mean, I didn't want to be found! How stupid am I? "Trixie," she says with finality. "Hi."

"Hi," I manage to squeak out. I anticipate the "You're coming with me, young lady" speech, but instead, I'm met with the round, tear-filled eyes of the woman.

She slides one of the papers across the glass countertop. I pick it up and examine it, but my brain isn't making the right connections. *Why is this private investigator handing me a piece of paper with June's picture on it?*

The picture is a Xerox copy of June's high school yearbook photo smack in the center. The word 'MISSING' is above the picture, and identifying features are below: "17 years old, 5' 5", blonde hair, blue eyes, 115 lbs., scar on her left ankle, call if you have any information."

June is missing? But I just saw her...

"What's this about?" I ask, keeping my gaze on June's face as the realization slowly sinks in that she's not here to take me away.

"I'm June's mother," she says against a hard lump in her throat. "She never came home from school on Monday."

"Wait," I say. "Aren't you a private investigator?"

Her face twists in confusion. It sounds so dumb even to my own ears. "No!" she squawks. "Did you hear what I said? June never came home!"

Silent tears stream down the woman's face like a sieve opening up. "What happened on Sunday when you last saw her? Did she say anything to you? Did she give you any indication of something weird going on?"

"June ran away?" I blurt and close my mouth tight right after as that was meant to be an inside thought.

"I don't know," she sighs heavily. "Did she talk about running away?"

I shake my head. "No! Absolutely not!" For that much I was certain. June had mentioned something about runaways in passing one night during our shift, and it actually had made me a little uncomfortable to open up to her. Like, I felt like she would have judged me if she had known the truth about where I had come from, which, in hindsight, was so dumb because I don't think June and Clark and Kent would have given a shit about my messed-up past. "June never said anything about being upset or planning on running away. No. Nothing. Sunday was a regular afternoon. We said goodbye when she got in Clark's car, and he took her home. I haven't talked to her since."

Her mother rests her forearms on the counter and bends the upper part of her body at her waist in exasperation. "Oh, God!" she cries. "Where the hell is my baby girl?"

I want to walk around and pat her on the back to try to give her some comfort, but I don't cause I'm actually very uncomfortable at the sight of this crying grown-up. I think of my own foster mother and how she probably wasn't half as distraught when she realized I had run away. "What did the cops say?"

She raises her head with a huff and in the dim light of the lobby, her eyes are rimmed with black desperation. "Give it time. She'll come back home. There's nothing we can do," she repeats what law enforcement has probably been telling her all week. "But this isn't like June. She wouldn't take off like that. She's very responsible, and things are good at home."

"I... I'm sorry. I don't know what to say."

"If you hear anything. See anything. Remember anything. Please, call me." She puts the stack of papers on the counter. "The manager said you could hang these up around the theatre for me. And take some to your school to hang up in case anyone knows anything."

"Sure. Sure. Of course," I say swooping the flyers up. *If only she knew there is no school…*

She wipes her face with her hands and does one last sniffle and smile before saying, "Thank you," and shuffling out of the lobby.

June? Missing? My mind starts going a mile a minute as I play out all the possibilities: *Did she actually run away, 'cause that seems like the most likely scenario? Was Carny John involved somehow? Did he stalk June as retribution for what happened with me?* I remember what Kent said a few weeks ago—*People sorta have a tendency to go missing in this town.* Was that what happened to June? Did she *vanish* into thin air? People don't just vanish into thin air! That's crazy talk!

An uneasy feeling comes over me, and I can't shake this unnerving sense of dread. June is my friend, and now she's gone. Maybe that's what Evelyn in Indianapolis is saying about me right now—*Trixie is my friend, and now she's gone.* Evelyn Markoff is a frumpy girl in my ceramics class who I would consider a "school friend" and not an "outside friend." But it's all the same when someone suddenly vanishes, I suppose. Friend, acquaintance, student, neighbor… when someone goes missing or dies, it doesn't matter what level of contact someone had with that person; the simple fact that someone in your life is "poof" crafts a special story that those people can now share together.

'Cause I vanished, didn't I?

But I had good reason to vanish. I was going to kill my foster father and quite possibly my foster mother, if she had tried to interfere. It was bound to happen; I just know it. That sonuvabitch had a heavy hand and a crass mouth, and there are only so many beatings a person can stand before they snap. I had dreamed up all the different ways I was going to enact my plan—all the different and delicious methods of torment and torture I had planned on inflicting upon him. Ultimately, it was going to be poison because there wouldn't be a whole lot of clean-up after, but it was Cyrinda who got into my subconscious and wormed her voice of reason into my brain. Murder was not in the cards for me, no matter how justified it was.

And June is my friend. Or at least that's what was starting to develop. A friendship, I suppose. 'Cause really, how well did I know her? We hadn't graduated past the "work-friend" stage yet, and for all I know, she could have had a super shitty life at home and just never mentioned it. Like I hadn't mentioned my own checkered history. Yet.

Apparently, Clark and Kent are distraught over this. They have been helping June's parents circulate flyers and organize searches all week. *Exactly, I haven't graduated to "actual friend" if this is the first I'm hearing about this.* By the way they talk, there's no way June would have run away. They swear up and down that she's the grooviest chick with the greatest life. And they would know, I mean, they've both known her for like forever forevers.

June's gone?

Vanished?

I can't wrap my head around it. The idea of it consumes my mind yet somehow propels me into autopilot mode. A secret part of me kinda curses June's name because I'm left stuck doing the job of two people. But I grin and bear it and push through the night. Well, I don't actually grin. I don't think I smile once the whole evening, and when Julius makes a snide comment to me about me not appearing friendly enough, I just stare him down. The whole night is a giant blur.

When my shift is over, I wipe my buttery hands down the front of my burgundy apron and wait for Ronnie to pick me up. Clark and Kent insist on staying with me until she gets there, and I can't help but think it's the sweetest, most protective thing anyone's done for me. *Maybe I am graduating to actual friend after all?* I tell them that if they need any help with the search to let me know—that I am heartbroken over the news (which, maybe I'm not *heartbroken*, per se, but I am definitely upset over it). They both get very serious, give me their phone numbers, and get this... they both *hug* me! Oh yeah, I just leveled up in the friend world.

I hop in the front seat when Ronnie arrives and scream in terror when Barbara whispers "Hello" from the back. My heart practically jumps into my throat as I wasn't expecting her to be there. She usually doesn't come with Ronnie to get me, and I hadn't noticed her when the car pulled up into the lot. Weird.

"Sorry, sorry," she says. "Didn't mean to frighten you."

Ronnie chuckles. "Yeah, but you did get her good!"

"I did, didn't I?" Barbara gives a little laugh in return. It's sweet like audio honey coating my ears, and I relax my shoulders.

"You are never going to believe this!" I blurt, anxious to get the tale of my missing friend into someone else's head.

"Shoot," Ronnie answers.

"My friend June. The girl that I work with. The girl who said she'd been to the Sisterhood meetings before. You know her, Ronnie. Or at least she said she knew you. Well, anyway, she's gone!"

"What do you mean she's gone?" Ronnie asks.

"Gone! Vanished! Poof! Her mother said she never came home from school on Monday. They're all putting up flyers and shit. Her mother came to the theatre today."

"Did she run away? You know that's so *en vogue* these days," and there's a slight sinister sarcasm in her comment.

I ignore it and tilt my body to look directly at Barbara in her form-fitting Wrangler jeans and sleeveless blue turtleneck. Her legs are crossed at the knees as one of her arms rests against the side console on the door, and the other is draped languidly across the back seat cushion. Half of her dark brown hair is tucked neatly behind her, while the other half hangs heavily over her shoulder. Her skin is so white, it almost glows—like she shimmers from the inside out. Like she's not really there. Like she's not real. "People sorta have a tendency to go missing in this town," she says, and I blink my eyes rapidly because I'm not sure if her mouth actually moved when she said it. Besides, that's what Kent said. Those were his exact words. There was no way she could have known.

"I'm sure she'll turn up," Ronnie says.

"That's what the fuzz keep telling her mom, but I can't help but think that this is all my fault."

"Your fault? How so?" Ronnie pries.

"Well," I hesitate, "last week. Carny John. He had been kinda sweet on June too. And well, after Barbara scared him away…"

Ronnie eyes Barbara in the rearview mirror, and for a split second, I get the feeling that they're somehow communicating with each other. But they can't be! That's impossible! I don't know, but they give each other a *knowing* kind of look. Almost like how when me and Cyrinda get vibes from each other, but there was definitely more to this glance.

"I'm sure your friend is fine," Barbara says with a sigh. "You shouldn't worry yourself with all that. And don't give that asshole Carny John another thought. We have bigger things to attend to tonight."

"Oh?" I say, and my ears perk up like a dog catching the scent of something.

"Remember when you first came to us I asked for your help with something I was working on?"

"Yes."

"Well, Trixie, tonight's the night. I need your help. Can I count on you?" Her eyes narrow, and in the reflection of the lights from the street, I swear they are dancing and laughing and changing color! They shift from brown to blue to green to gold to white to the darkest black all in the matter of seconds.

"Of course you can," I say, but the words never leave my lips because I'm still mesmerized by Barbara's kaleidoscope eyes.

Chapter Nine

Friday, April 23rd 1965
Barbara Thorne's House
163 North Shelby Avenue
Salem, Illinois
Night of the Half Moon

Back at the house, Ronnie and Barbara lead me into the back den—the place where my first Sisterhood meeting was held. I pause for a second as I pass my bedroom, hesitating on whether or not I should check on Cyrinda, but Ronnie grabs hold of my arm at the elbow and propels me forward. Cyrinda is sick anyway. She's probably been resting all day, and I really shouldn't disturb her. Besides, Barbara asked for *me*—for *my* help! The thought of being wanted and needed by her makes me feel special, and that's something that is on me and me alone. I kinda like having something for myself for once.

Candlelight glows throughout, and the furniture is pushed against the walls to make space in the center of the room. A woman in a black hooded cape sits inside a pentagram made with coarse salt. In her lap is a white canvas, (like one of those ones you paint portraits on) and a sketching pencil. I recognize the materials because we used similar tools in my art class in Indianapolis. A black candle flickers in the center of the circle next to a chalice of wine and a knife with engravings on its hilt. At every point of the star, another black candle casts shadows on the woman's face. What the hood doesn't cover, her dark hair conceals, and I have trouble making out her features. And in the darkness of the room, I can't tell if her hair is black like Ronnie's or brown like Barbara's. She hums and mums something, and my ears pick up on music being played somewhere. Like the night I saw Ronnie and Barbara together on the bed. *But that didn't* really *happen, did it?*

"Is this a Sisterhood meeting?" I ask Barbara as she escorts me to sit in between two points of the pentagram. Barbara sits to my left and Ronnie sits to my right, and the woman is next to Barbara. There's an empty spot in between the bottom parts of the star, and for a second I think it could be a spot for Cyrinda. I want to ask if I can wake her up and bring her in, but Barbara interrupts my flow of thinking. *Better yet, this is just for me.*

"No, Trixie," she answers, "this is something different."

"Your project?"

"Yes. My project." Barbara takes the chalice from the center of the circle, drinks deep, and passes it to me. I take a sip. It's the same sour-tasting brew she gave us on our first night here.

The metallic taste grabs me at the back of my throat, and I try hard to stifle a cough before passing it to Ronnie. Unaffected by its taste, she drinks from the cup and places it back in the center of the star. I find it odd that she never offered any to the mysterious woman who sits among us.

Barbara then reaches her hand to grab mine and juts her chin so that I hold on to Ronnie's with my other hand. The woman at the other point of the circle begins drawing on the canvas with the pencil, her gentle scribbles work in time with music that has somehow amplified in my head.

The candles, the wine, the woman cloaked in black… why if I had my doubts about it before, they are definitely squashed now—this is a full-on witch ritual unlike anything I'd ever seen on that television show *Bewitched* or read about in that play *The Crucible*.

"We come together in this circle in perfect love and perfect trust," Barbara begins, and she squeezes my hand. Unsure of how to respond, I squeeze Ronnie's.

"Blessed be," Ronnie says.

Again, I'm unsure of myself, and I end up muttering some version of what Ronnie said.

Barbara raises our clasped hands in the air. "Tonight, under the light of the half-moon, we accept our new sister, Patricia Bluebell McGovern, into our home and circle. Sent to us by your son, sent to us by our brother the Silver Locust, we welcome Trixie with open hearts and open minds and open souls."

My head swims. The wine and the music root their way into my consciousness, and the air in the room gets heavy. Hot. No, not hot. Thick. The air is thick with incense and candle smoke, and moisture, and fog, and I can't make sense of what my thoughts are trying to tell me.

"Trixie," Ronnie says, "Barbara is inviting you to be a part of our group—to be a part of us. Is that what you would like?"

Be part of them? Be part of something? Be someone without Cyrinda there? Be my own self, my own person? Those thoughts had scarcely ever invaded my mind, and the concept now is kinda mind-bending. I nod at her.

She smiles. "Good. Barbara will ask you a series of questions. Nod to her if you understand. Respond 'In perfect love and perfect trust' when she is done. Do you understand?"

"Yes, I understand completely!" I want to exclaim, but my lips only press themselves together in an acknowledging hum.

Barbara squeezes my hand, and I turn to face her. "Trixie, be not afraid. I will go before you always. I have chosen you to join us in our circle. From the moment you came to me, I knew you were special. But I need you to affirm to me that you are with us of your own free will and that you want to be a part of our special movement."

I nod in agreement.

Barbara smiles and her perfectly white teeth shine in the candlelight, and the shadows in the room make it look like she has two faces for a split second. Like how I remember Trent's face looking in his car all those weeks ago. "Do you, Trixie, accept the gift of sisterhood to be valued, and cherished, and protected? Do you swear to follow the ways and abide by the governing laws of the Sisterhood? Do you give of yourself freely and openly to our cause? Are you willing to respect and support your sisters, nurturing the bonds of trust and unity within our sacred circle? Will you embrace the cycles of life, acknowledging the phases of the Maiden, the Mother, and the Crone, within you and in others?"

The music gets louder—it's a steady beat with a steady drum, and it reminds me of the hippie songs at the park when they would gather around together and smoke grass and hold hands and praise the earth. The voices of the song try to harmonize, but they don't do a very good job of it— it's disjointed words and notes that are jumbled and garbled together in some weird mish-mosh. I try desperately to train my ears to one particular voice that sounds like a mezzo-soprano male. I try to isolate his vocals from the others so I can at least understand something that is being sung.

My back stiffens when I hear it. *Say you love Satan.* His voice calls out to me over the thrumming of the music. *Say you love Satan.* But it sounded so far away like he said it in another time zone or something. The words feel dangerous—forbidden. And I can't help but get a jolt of satisfaction from the naughtiness of it all. The secretiveness of it all. This type of stuff only happens in movies and adult books, and here I am—saying I love Satan in my head, liking the way it makes me feel.

"Do you, Trixie?" Barbara urges me to answer, drawing me away from the song.

I focus my attention back on Barbara. Her eyes have turned green. "In perfect love and perfect trust," I say. In my head, it sounded confident and sure, but what actually came out was much to be desired.

Barbara smiles at me. "Gathered under the gentle light of the Moon, we are now united within our sacred circle. Sisters new, and those who have journeyed with us before, we come together as one, committed to our shared purpose until our work is complete."

"Blessed be," Ronnie replies.

"Blessed be," Barbara says.

Ronnie squeezes my hand, and I reply with the same refrain, yet the mysterious woman in the circle makes no response and continues to scribble on the canvas. "What is the work we are going to complete?" I ask, and Barbara and Ronnie eye each other sharply and release their grip on me.

Barbara folds her hands into her lap and sighs. "I'm so glad you asked that," she says. "I have waited so long for you, and now that you are here, I don't know how or where to start."

"I... I don't understand," I stammer, confused. I have to admit, I'm a little afraid. How is it possible that she's waited for *me*? I barely know her.

Yes, I'm drawn to her magnetic presence, but she's just the woman who took us in temporarily.

"I know it feels that way," she says as if reading my mind, "but I promise you, you have a purpose so much larger than yourself. There's a reason you left your home in Indianapolis. There's a reason why you just so happened to get into Galen's car."

Trent, I think to myself.

"Of course. Trent," she says gently, and my skin breaks out in goosebumps. "There's a bigger picture that you are about to play a major role in, and I am *bursting* with excitement for what's to come." She smiles wide again. It's genuine and true, not one of these fakey-fake smiles I have to give to the faceless, nameless customers at the movie house. "You're quitting that job, by the way. There's no need for you to…"

"Wait," I say, confused again, "I can't quit. I have to make some money so we can eventually get our own place and…"

She shakes her head violently back and forth. "No, ma'am. Put all that aside and just listen to me. I told you, you have a bigger purpose. All the minutia of the day-to-day," she waves her hand in the air in a dismissive gesture, "it doesn't matter in the grand scheme of things."

"So, just what *is* the grand scheme of things?"

She inhales deeply, her chest rises like a balloon being inflated. I can't tell if she's annoyed with me and my questions, and that makes me anxious. I feel out of place. I don't know what

I'm doing or what I've gotten myself into, and before I can think another self-conscious thought, the woman scribbling on the canvas suddenly stops and gasps. Barbara's eyes flash wide for a second, and she cranes her neck over to look at the drawing. Like a giddy schoolgirl, her shoulders rise up and down in quick spurts, and she lets out a little giggle.

"There's not much time, so I will condense this as much as I can for you. A very long time ago I had two children—a boy and a girl. Twins. My sweet, precious babies. Gretchen and David. But they were taken away from me by some very bad people, and they were murdered. Burned alive. I've kept their ashes with me ever since. I take them wherever I go because I know one day they will return to me. One day I will bring them back in the flesh so we can be a family again."

My back stiffens, and I make a croaking sound in my throat. A wave of fear overcomes me because I think this has got to be the craziest thing I've ever heard. Getting beat-downs from my foster father doesn't seem so bad right about now...

Ronnie puts a hand on my shoulder. "Trust me. I had the same reaction when she told me, too. It seems crazy. It seems unbelievable. But I promise you, I've seen Barbara do things that can't be explained. She's the real deal, Trixie. The genuine article. She has great power. You know it. You saw it too."

Carny John.

Barbara nods at her to acknowledge her words. "I traveled the world over seeking guidance from different teachers. I searched everywhere for someone to give me the answers to the questions I sought. I knew I had the power inside me to make the children whole again, but it was a matter of time, place, moon phase, words, elements, and everything in between. See, I am from the blood of an ancient one called Blodwyn. It is said that Blodwyn had the power to resurrect the dead—the only magic worker to have the power to do so. Blodwyn raised her dead so I could raise mine." She pauses and motions to the hooded woman in the circle. "This is Arrah. She is from the old country, the place of Blodwyn's birth. I found her many years ago in an icy cave in the North—a region called the Frostheim Forest. Arrah is a heksa…"

"Blodheksa?" I blurt out, interrupting her.

Arrah stops drawing and looks up at me as a heavy silence blankets the room. The pencil falls from her hand, and as she reaches to pick it up, I notice the tips of her fingers are black as if she'd dipped them in paint. Barbara's eyes darken scarily for a moment. In that split second, she is not Barbara anymore, but a flash of white light and ancient symbols. *Blodwyn?* It was only for a fleeting moment, and when the visage of Barbara returns, she puts a gentle hand on my knee, and her face softens again. "No, Trixie, that's something entirely different. Arrah sees things and knows things, and she can commune with the dead and lost souls."

"A witch?" I blurt again.

"Something like that. The word 'witch' has been so diluted over the ages, though. It's been bastardized and demonized and parodied forward and backward."

Ronnie coughs a fake cough, and through the noise, she says the name "Samantha Stephens" — the main character from that show *Bewitched*. Barbara gives a slight smirk and a half-eye roll and ignores her comment.

"But 'heksa?'" Barbara continues. "That word is for us. The true ones. The pure ones. The ones who walk the outskirts of the veil."

"Is Trent a heksa?"

"As a matter of fact, he is. A very strong one. Important. Key. Different than the rest, but like me. A heksa all the same."

"But he's a boy! Aren't guys warlocks?"

Ronnie swats me on the arm. "Total misnomer. Though rare, men can be heksas just as much as women can be. A warlock is totally a made-up thing with no basis in…"

I quickly turn my head from her and look back at Barbara. "Is Ronnie a heksa?" I ask, excitedly. I feel like some unknown, previously unsought wellspring of knowledge has just presented itself to me and I'm trying to absorb every last bit of information.

"No. Like I told you, Ronnie is an associate. An acolyte. She's a loyal follower of the cause. When the dawn of the New Eden comes to fruition, all heksas and their acolytes will be saved from the carnage and will live freely in paradise."

"New Eden?" I ask, and my voice uncontrollably cracks as the fuzziness of it all once again sets in.

"In time," Ronnie says, rubbing my back. "I know, it's a lot to take in. You'll understand soon enough."

"Wait! Am *I* an acolyte?" I croak.

Barbara closes her eyes in content. "No, Trixie," she exclaims and the jubilance in her voice echoes like a symphony in the room. "You are so much more!"

Ronnie removes her hand from my back, and I glance at her. Her face has completely changed and her demeanor toward me has shifted. Suddenly, she makes me feel uncomfortable. Something in Barbara's words stabbed her deep.

Barbara turns my chin to face her. "There's a light inside of you that shines so boldly and so brightly. When I first saw you, I felt like I had to squint to make out the features of your face. You are pure. Golden. So golden that you reflect the veil that hangs between this world and the next. When I look at you, I can see the stars moving in the sky. I can see the mouth of the otherworld open its jaws and try to let our old ancestors through to claim their rightful dominion over this world. You are blessed. Sacred. And those who are like me..."

"Heksas?"

She nods. "They can see it too. But others…"

"Like Ronnie?"

She nods. "Even though they can't see the actual light shining from you like I can, they know it's there. They can sense it. That's why people are so drawn to you. Attracted to you. Like June. Like the boy you worked with. Like that Carny John kid. Like so many others in your life over the years, I'm sure. Those who are evil, or who want to derail our ultimate goal, will try to abuse that light, and steal it for themselves."

"Like my foster dad?"

She nods. "And Carny John. So now, with you here with me, I can protect that light—*we* can protect that light. Keep it pure. Keep it safe. Galen sent you to me because he knew you were the one who could help me bring back the twins. And, Trixie, I can't begin to express to you how very important they are to lifting the veil—to opening the gash in the sky. It can't be done without them. And there's only so much of *them* that I have left. The box of their ashes won't last forever, for as the years move on, and I keep trying to resurrect them, my failed attempts dwindle the remnants of them."

"So how are you planning on… how are we going to…?"

Barbara raises a hand to silence me and extends her other long arm to Arrah. Arrah tugs Barbara's hand with the palm side up and brings her fingers to her mouth. She opens up wide, revealing her two sharp canine teeth like the fangs of a snake, and bites down on the tip. Barbara squirms for a second as Arrah suckles hungrily. She makes a delighted, gurgling sound before Barbara pulls her hand back. Arrah picks the pencil back up and continues her sketch.

Barbara takes the knife from the center of the circle and motions for me to give her my hand. "Stay still," she says. "The athame will only hurt you if you are not willing to give yourself over one hundred percent. It is very old and has many a song to sing." With that, the music in the room seems to get louder, and Barbara makes a small slice in my forefinger. Just as she had said, there is no pain. The cut felt like the wings of a locust brushing lightly against my hand. I stare as my blood blooms to the surface of my skin, and instinctually, I want to raise it to my mouth to stop the blood from flowing. "Uh-uh," she admonishes and hands me the knife. "You must cut Ronnie."

I take it from her, and mimicking her actions, I make a similar small cut on Ronnie's finger and place the knife back in the circle.

"Under the ancient tapestry of stars, amidst the whispers of the Black Wood forest, and the radiant gaze of the Half Moon. What transpires in our circle is an act of profound commitment and unity, a bond forged in the most sacred and primal way—through the mixing of our blood." Ronnie presses her finger onto mine as a line of our blood trickles down to our wrists. I don't know where her blood ends and my blood begins because it is now one—one flow, one stream, one connection.

"By Earth and moon, our souls entwine. In sacred sisterhood, our spirits shine. With blood we bind, with love we guide. In our coven's circle, we shall abide," Ronnie chants, and her words flow so perfectly with the disharmonious music in the background that I can't help but wonder if she hears it too. It seems to come so naturally to her like she's done this before.

With Barbara.

Then again, Ronnie's done a lot of other things with Barbara, too, and suddenly I think: *Will that be expected of me?*

As if breaking into my thoughts, Barbara takes my hand, stopping the blood flow of me and Ronnie. "Freely offered and freely accepted, this symbolizes an unbreakable connection. It is a testament of your trust, your devotion. Just as the rivers merge into one vast sea, you have merged your essence into the collective consciousness of our sacred coven. The Crimson Coven. Bound in blood. Above and beyond the scope of the Sisterhood." She presses the open wound on her finger into mine, and something like an explosion goes off in my brain.

I close my eyes for a second, and when I open them again, I am no longer in the den in Barbara's house. I am no longer in the circle with the other women. I am floating. Floating. Flying in the midnight blue sky. Flying amongst the stars. They twinkle like shimmering glitter. So many of them—too many to count. But they all have names. Every one of them has a name I can't pronounce or repeat or understand, but as Barbara's blood seeps onto and into my skin like burning matches scorching my hand, the stars tell me their names. I think one is called Josephine, but I can't be sure.

I want more. I want to feel more. I want to see more. So, I grab Barbara's hand and bring her finger to my lips and suckle the way Arrah did. Suddenly, my vision shifts, brightens. It's as if her blood is pure light seeping into my body and changing my vantage point. It makes me squint as the darkness of the candlelit room is no more. It's as bright as the brightest day, like sunlight filtering through from behind the walls. I can see. I can see everything!

She's drugged me, I think as a wave of euphoria crashes into my chest and lifts me higher into the sky. I look down at the house beneath me, and I can see through the roof and the walls. I see the bedroom where I stay, but Cyrinda is not there. She doesn't sleep. She doesn't rest. And I panic when I think she's left me!

Be not afraid. She doesn't exist in this realm, a voice says beneath the drumming beat of the music, and my heart aches for a second at the thought of her not being with me.

She is not one of us, the voice says. It's gravelly and guttural. Like rocks on the pavement crunching under the weight of a tractor-trailer. A tractor-trailer traveling at high speed across the open highway so it can pick up the Blodheksa and fuck her all night long.

I rub my temple with my free hand because my thoughts don't make any sense. They are jumbled and disjointed, like the voices singing in the song. Singing in the sky. Like the stars with names like Aizel and Aroviak. Disjointed with images of things that have happened in the past, things happening right now, and things yet to come. Barbara's blood inches its way into me. It is sweet. Divine. It tickles. Makes the crevice between my legs laugh. Ronnie plays with my sex—her fingers tap the outer fleshy areas of me. But how could she be doing that when I'm in the sky, dancing among the stars with crazy names like Evanak and Braylaxis. Whatever she's doing to me makes me cum. Over and over and over again, or maybe it's just one never-ending orgasm? Yes! It is! It doesn't stop. I cum hard and fast and in a continuous loop. My juices flood the world beneath me, and the house fills with my squishy orgasm like a tidal wave sweeping it out to my orgasmic sea. Cyrinda drowns in it too. But they said she doesn't exist. The children said she's not with me in this realm.

I hear children giggle in the distance. It's muffled beneath the music at first, but it quickly grows louder. Back in the circle, Barbara and Ronnie cheer. Barbara releases her fingers from my mouth, and I feel as if I tumble back to Earth. I awaken and watch as Barbara squeezes her finger over the canvas, letting her blood drip all over Arrah's drawing. As my eyes start to shift into focus, a bright light surrounds the canvas in Barbara's lap. "They are ten," Arrah says to Barbara in a gravelly voice. "The right number. And that is how they shall stay."

Barbara nods as if she understands. I'm glad she does because I have no idea what any of this means. But it's obvious it's important to Barbara. She beams. She glows. She holds up the canvas and the white light sucks itself into the canvas. In its place is a portrait—an oil painting of two children: one boy, one girl, with black hair and smoky gray eyes. Dressed in an old-fashioned pinafore and little boy suit, they hug each other in the picture. Brother and sister with sideways smiles on their faces. They look familiar. Like Barbara, yes, but also like someone else I've known. Like the stars in the sky when I floated among them. *No, that can't be right.*

Like Trent?

Be not afraid, a voice echoes in my head.

Trent's voice. Trent's song. Assuring me. Guiding me. Reminding me to...

"Keep your good thoughts flowing and your actions to match," Ronnie says with a giant smile plastered on her face. Did she hear his voice, too?

I can't help but stare at the painting—the details in it, the realism of it. It's almost as if the twins are going to jump out of the picture at any second! They laugh again, and I swear the little girl turns to look at me. Her tight-lipped smile reminds me of a secret—of a smile given in thanks.

And somehow I come to understand—I don't know how or why, but I just know that it wasn't only Barbara's blood that stirred the drawing to semi-life. I played a part in this too.

The Crimson Coven. Bound in blood.

Sheepishly, I smile back and give a small wave to the little girl, and her laughter fills the room, drowning out the last echoes of the music and drowning out the hoots and hollers from Barbara.

Chapter Ten

Saturday, May 1st 1965
The Bus Stop on Main Street
Salem, Illinois
Night of the New Moon

When I told Cyrinda about my initiation and what I had participated in and witnessed, she was not on board with any of it. But I basically told her that she had zero to say and that she needed to mind her own business.

"But you are my business," she had cried.

I ignored her tears. Chalked them up to her jealousy that I was part of something that she wasn't. "Barbara chose *me* for something, not you!" I scolded her defensively, to which she cowered on the bed like a weak, beat-up puppy dog. "Besides, none of this would even be possible without me! I made the plan. I got the courage to run away. I got a job to try to secure our futures. And what did you do? Got sick and stayed in bed? What did you contribute but stress and anxiety! Maybe I don't want a shadow anymore."

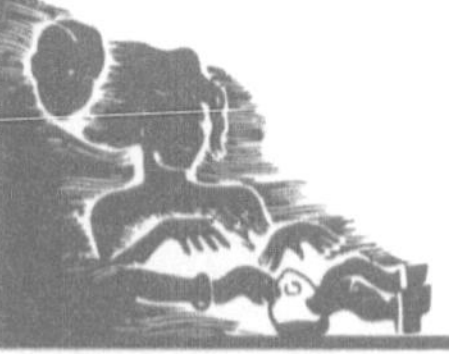

"Why are you saying these things to me, Trixie?" she wailed. "Why are you acting so cruel? We're supposed to be a team. We've always been a team!"

"Well maybe that needs to change," I said callously and watched in disgust as her tears streamed down her face.

"I'm feeling better!" she pleaded. "See, I'll be up in no time, and I can come work with you at the movie theatre since that girl has been missing."

"It's no use now," I bark. "I quit. Barbara needs my full attention. If you want to go down to the theatre and ask Julius for a job, then fine, but I don't work there anymore."

Cyrinda's eyes went wide like they usually do when she's scared or nervous. I swear, I wanted to pluck them out of her face and squash them between my fingers! "No, Trix!" she exclaimed. "We were supposed to save up to get out of here."

"Yes, I know. *We* were. But then that became *me*. And I realized that I'm in this alone. You haven't done anything for me but give me grief." I paused for the drama of it. "Always. All the time. Every waking moment we're together."

She put her hands up to her face and silently sobbed into them. "Why are you saying this?" she cried in muffled pants. "It's this place! It's this place! We shouldn't be here."

"And that's exactly why Barbara doesn't want you in the Sisterhood. That's why Barbara doesn't want you in the Crimson Coven."

"The Crimson Coven? What even is that? What kind of witchy, voodoo shit is she making you do? Please, Trixie. Let's just go. Let's just forget about all of this while we still have the chance."

"Oh yeah?" I scoffed. "And go where? Back home? Back to where we came from?"

She shrugged her shoulders and lowered her head. "I don't know. Anywhere but here. It feels like this place is changing you."

"What does that even mean?" I growled.

"This place," she said, and she motioned her hands above her head in an arch to express the entirety of the room. "All of it. Doesn't it feel off to you? Like, something doesn't jive. Sometimes I walk around when I'm all alone…"

"Snooping?" I barked, cutting her off.

"No. Just getting up and stretching my legs is all. But sometimes, I think I hear music. I can't explain it, but I know there can't really be music playing because everyone is out for the day, but still, it's there. Like it's underneath the surface."

"Of the house?" I scoffed. "That's ridiculous!"

"Not literally underneath the house, Trixie! That's not what I mean. It's like there are layers in the atmosphere or something. Hiding something. Concealing something. Something underneath, and not the foundation. But yes, the foundation," she paused and thought on her play-on-words for a moment. "Things look fuzzy here. Feel fuzzy. Things shift in the shadows, and the books on the shelves have titles and pages that I can't under-stand or read. Witch stuff."

"Witch stuff? Have you lost your mind?" I crowed condescendingly.

"No ma'am. Have you?"

"I don't know, Cyri. You're talking a little cuckoo right now."

"I swear to you, Trixie. I went into the den the other day and picked up a copy of *Dr. Bloodmoney*. Only, it wasn't *Dr. Bloodmoney*. The pages felt weird and when I opened it, there were words on the pages, but they weren't words that I could discern. The word Bloodmoney looked odd, too. Out of place. Like Blood-something, but I can't remember. As a matter of fact, the more I stared at all the words, the more my eyes went blurry and out of focus."

Her words struck me in the chest because I knew exactly what she was talking about—the music, the books, the blood-soaked lovefest with the mirror and weird portal. *And the Crimson Coven ceremony...* But again, I poo-pooed her claims and blew air from my mouth dismissively. "You're exaggerating. It was probably an international copy of the book. Like, in another language."

She hung her head down so low her chin touched her chest. "The fact that you're not even listening to me tells me you've changed."

"No, Cyrinda. I haven't changed. For the first time in my life, I feel safe. I feel wanted. I feel accepted. I feel loved."

Quickly, she shot up on her knees on the bed and frantically reached for me, like to pull me closer to her, to make me feel her words. "*I love you, Trixie. I accept you.*"

I pulled away and turned my back from her. For a split second, my heart had softened, and I felt bad for the things I had said. "That's different. It's not the same."

"I'm begging you! Please! Let's just take our things and go. I'm better now. We can both work. There's gotta be a shelter or somewhere else we can stay for a while. What she wants you to do is not right. It doesn't sound right. It doesn't feel right. Why does it have to be you? Why do you have to bring in recruits for her Sisterhood group?"

Because you are the light, and the truth, and the way, a voice called to me, but I can't be sure if I even heard it or not.

"Like I said," I finally replied, "you can go ask Julius for my job, but I need to see this through. I promised Barbara I would help her find new recruits for the Sisterhood. She needs me." And I walked out the door, and in my mind's eye, Cyrinda collapsed into a heap of endless sobs on the bed.

Which brings me to now.

The green iron bench at the bus stop.

An unusually chilly spring night.

The streetlamp buzzing in and out of consciousness as if it's playing on some kind of loop or timer.

I have no idea how I am going to do this, but I am determined.

I glance down at my watch. 8:15 p.m. it reads. Ronnie said the bus should get here around 8:20-ish. It's the busy bus—the one with all the people filtering in from the city. But this is the last connector stop, the one that will take any of the lingering lost souls further out west. West of here. More west than where they started out.

I was a lost soul once upon a time, but I didn't get on a bus, 'cause buses cost money.

Before I get a chance to get all introspective, the bus screeches to a crunching stop at the corner, the brakes on the beast sound as if they're going to tear right through the guts of the machine. I try not to be too conspicuous when the door hisses open and the people start filing out. I run my fingers through my hair and look up and down Main Street as if I'm searching for someone—waiting for someone.

'Cause I kinda am.

The second she bounces off the bus—I know it's her. A lost soul. A wandering spirit. She throws a yellow duffle bag over her shoulder, and I think that's what I must have looked like just a short time ago. She's got the fresh-runaway look plastered all over her freckled face, and I pray to God she takes a seat at the bench next to me. As the doors close tight and the bus noisily pulls away, the girl takes out a bus schedule from her back pocket, runs a long finger down to the bottom, reads the presumed new pick-up times, and saunters over to the green iron bench.

"Hi," I say nonchalantly, and I shimmy over to unconsciously give her the "okay" to sit next to me.

She smiles back, takes the bait, and sits down. She places her bag on the ground in front of her and loops her foot through the strap to make sure her belongings are secure.

"Hi," she says back with a little crack in her voice. Her nervousness comes off her like steam from the asphalt on a hot summer day.

"I'm Trixie."

She looks at me and a glint of suspicion twinkles in her soft blue eyes, like she somehow knows that's not my real name. Even though it kinda is. "Donna."

"You getting the transfer, Donna?" I ask.

"Oh, yeah, yeah," she says folding up the schedule and placing it in her lap.

"Where you headed?"

She tucks her curly chestnut hair behind her ears, and I notice her earlobes go red with embarrassment. She sucks in her lower lip and breathes slowly. "Probably California."

"Probably?"

"Yeah. Probably. You?"

"Oh, I'm here waiting for a ride."

"Oh, groovy," she says in a faraway voice.

"Why California?"

She shrugs. "Why not?"

"Sure. Why not." I pause, picking my next words carefully. "I was gonna head out to Cali too, but it seems like everyone is going that way.

Girls way prettier than me thinking they're gonna be the next Marilyn or something. I didn't stand a chance."

Donna nervously curls the edges of the schedule. She is fresh—like lemonade on a hot summer day, only it's not summer yet, and a cold breeze fills the space between us on the bench. She tucks her hands underneath her armpits to shield them from the bite in the air. "Yeah," she drones, and I get the sense she's questioning her own intentions right about now. Donna is very pretty, there's no doubt about that, and she can't be a day over nineteen. But she's alone, and afraid, and I think I just threw a wrench of doubt in her life plan.

A flyer stapled to the telephone pole rustles in the wind, and I glance over at it. The face in the black and white picture stares at me with a cheerful, cheerleader smile. *June.* For a split second, I feel kinda bad cause I had started to forget about her. Two weeks and already she's the furthest thing from my mind. In the picture she looks so bubbly, so innocent, so perfect—her mother chose a good photo to represent her. I think of my own Missing Person Flyer. Am I in the local police station? Grocery store? Movie theatre? Telephone pole? Did my foster mom pick out a nice picture of me, or is it some lame one with a silly look on my face? Maybe it's that dumb picture she has of me reading a book at the community pool. She had called my name, I looked up for a quick second with my mouth agape and *click!* Picture taken! I was so mad at her for that one.

Donna catches me staring at the flyer and asks, "Who's that?"

"That's June. She was a friend of mine," I say, heavily laying on the drama because June is now officially a part of my story—the one that people share and commiserate over. The one that binds people together. *Hey! I don't know you, but we both knew June so…* "Gone almost two weeks now," I say forlornly.

Two weeks, and the farthest thing from my mind.

Donna makes a little gasp. "That's terrible. Did she run away?"

I shrug. "No one knows. There aren't any leads. It's like she just vanished."

"People don't just vanish!" Donna exclaims.

"I did. I'm guessing you did too."

She purses her lips together and grimaces. "I guess you're right."

"What time is the transfer coming?" I ask.

She fumbles with the paper and checks the schedule. "Not 'til 10 p.m.," she says, and a tinge of panic rises in her voice.

"Hmmm," I mumble thoughtfully.

"Hmmm, what?" she repeats.

"It's just that ten's late to be out here alone. My ride will be here soon and…"

A car suddenly turns the corner and pulls up to the curb, preventing me from finishing my thought.

"That your ride?" Donna asks as the window rolls down.

"Oh no. Definitely not my ride."

Clark leans over the front seat so his head is almost to the passenger side window. "Trixie?" he asks, surprised. "I thought that was you! What happened? Where have you been?"

Through the thick windshield of his car, his eyes give a little glimmer under the thin light of the streetlamp. I remember how I thought he was attractive when I first met him. How my knees knocked a little when he brushed up beside me. How I had wanted to hang out with the gang so badly just so I could get to know him better…

"I quit, Clark. I had to. I couldn't bear it," I lie.

"I know what you mean," he says, hanging his head low for a reflective moment. "I thought we lost you, too."

"Nope. Still here. Still kicking."

"Good, good."

"Any word on June? Anything new?"

"Nothing. Cops are still saying she's a runaway."

"Fuck! Well, keep me posted if you hear anything."

"Will do. Hey, Trixie. You should come by the theatre to pick up some more of June's flyers. Or we could go over to Centralia and put some up together. Call me. I told June's mom to put my number on the poster if there were any tips."

I fidget and wring my hands together nervously. My knees get that shaky feeling in them,

and I practically stutter over my words. "Uh…
yyy… yyyeah. Sure."

"Groovy." He looks in his rearview mirror
and turns his head side to side looking up and
down Main Street. "Hey, you shouldn't be out
here alone. Do you need a ride?"

"No, Clark. I'm fine, thank you. Ronnie will
be here soon."

He pauses, hesitates, then puts up two fingers in the peace sign and drives away. I look at
Donna who is as white as a ghost. "You okay?" I
ask, feigning concern.

"Yeah, um, is this like a bad part of town or
something?"

I twist the side of my mouth and groan a little.
"Depends on who you ask."

She bends forward, unwraps the strap of her
bag from her ankle, and brings it up to her chest
like a security blanket. "When did you say your
ride was getting here?"

"Soon."

"I see," she says, defeated, and looks to
the ground.

I breathe in deeply, creating an awkward
silence between us. A gust of air blows again,
harder this time—colder—and I sense Donna's
ever-growing concern. It mounts. Builds.
Flourishes in the space between us. Permeates
throughout the moonless, midnight blue sky.
Rattles my every last nerve. Until finally I exhale
loudly. "Look," I begin, "I'm staying somewhere

real safe. Just me and a few other girls. Why don't you come back with me tonight."

She tenses up and her eyes darken.

"We'll have something to eat, and I'll get Rhonda to drive you back here first thing in the morning to catch the early bus."

"I… I don't know…"

I reach my hand over and touch the top of her knee. "Barbara helped me. She took me and a friend of mine in about a month ago. She can help you too."

I can see by the look on her face that she wrestles with the idea. She had been so cautious, so careful not to get into a car with strangers, and here she is, on the last leg of her journey contemplating doing the very thing she'd avoided all this time. The wind howls just as Ronnie pulls up. Her eyes go wide with fear at the prospect of me leaving her alone in the dark in this big bad town. June's flyer rattles wildly against its staples like bat wings echoing in a cave.

"That's my ride," I say, jumping up to my feet. "It was nice meeting you, Donna. Stay safe out here. I hope you make it out to Cali okay." And I start walking over to the Ford.

As I'm about to open the door, Donna quickly stands up and calls my name. "Hey, Trixie? Offer still good?"

I put up a finger as if to tell her to wait one second and dip my head into the car.

"Is she *her*?" Ronnie asks.

"I think so."

Ronnie looks over my shoulder, grazes her eyes up and down Donna's form in the distance, and nods. I twist the upper half of my body to look back at her. I give her the thumbs up, and a smile of relief sweeps across her face as she hustles over and slithers into the backseat.

"Thank you guys so much," she gushes.

"Our pleasure," Ronnie answers, and she drives back to the house.

Chapter Eleven

Saturday, May 1st 1965
Barbara Thorne's House
163 North Shelby Avenue
Salem, Illinois
Night of the New Moon

The chain on the lightbulb flails violently in place when Ronnie tugs on it to light our way into the basement. It clanks gently on the bulb and makes a faint echo-y noise against the concrete walls. I have never been down here—I actually didn't realize there was a basement until tonight. It smells damp, weathered, and a metallic scent wafts just underneath that moldy, musty smell. "Watch your step," Ronnie says, guiding me down the stairs, but I don't need the light. Since my vision had shifted the night we did the ritual of the Crimson Coven, seeing in the dark seems easier for me somehow.

I suspect Ronnie needs it, though.

And Donna does too.

In the middle of the room, Donna stirs awake as we approach. Her beautiful brown hair now matted into sticky clumps on her forehead. Her eyes flutter open, and when the realization of her mouth gag and hand and feet restraints become a reality, they go wide and wild and she tries so hard to speak, to shout, to scream. The cloth gag silences her, and every would-be word is muffled against the fabric and her stationary tongue.

"Ih-cksy! Ih-cksy!" she tries to say my name, to get my attention.

"Calm down," Ronnie commands her.

Donna uses all her strength to try to hoist herself off the metal folding chair. She is able to move it about an inch to the left and almost tumbles over to her side. Ronnie's face darkens with anger, and she quickly makes a long stride over to Donna. She forcefully puts her hands on Donna's shoulders, locking her in place. They are delicately large. Manly, but not. Soft, but not. Short, manicured nails dig into Donna's clothes. "No more of that!" Ronnie yells. "If you keep this up, I'll have to sedate you again."

Scared and shaken, Donna relaxes her body and tries to settle herself down, but her tears are a constant stream down the sides of her cheeks. A deluge of terror and confusion.

Ronnie reaches into her back jeans pocket and pulls out a piece of white chalk. "Draw the star in the circle on the floor," she instructs.

The gray cement is stained. Black. Brown. Red. Oil stains. Wine stains. Blood stains. Body stains. It all becomes clearer as I kneel down to write on the ground. Splatters and splashes light up like spilled paint splotches, and I think: *They've done this before. This has happened before.* My stomach flips over, and I feel like I'm going to hurl. I gag in my throat. Vomit rises.

"Oh, cut it out!" Ronnie chastises. "It's fine."

"It's fine. It's fine," I repeat, drawing the circle.

Ronnie walks over to a workbench on the other side of the room and pulls out a box from one of the drawers. Inside is an old-looking leather book and a bundle—something wrapped in what looks like deer skin. She unravels it to reveal the knife—what Barbara had called the ceremonial athame. Ronnie pulls it out and dangles it in front of her face, mesmerized. Donna frantically shakes against her restraints. She bucks and moans something that resembles "Ell-lf! "Ell-lf!"

Help me. What else can she try to say?

"That's what Barbara used the other night," I say with confidence, ignoring Donna's plea.

Ronnie nods, then grips the jeweled hilt in her palm and points the blade at Donna. "Shut the fuck up, or I will kill you right here and now!" she screams angrily. Donna's muffled sobs of agony grow louder even though she struggles to not make a sound.

"Ronnie!" I beg, and she turns back to me.

She turns the knife over, inspecting it. "It's old, Trixie," she says. "Barbara told me how Galen kind of like initiated her with it back in the day. She said it has tremendous power."

"Can you feel it?" I ask, staring at the way her wrist turns side to side.

"It's heavy, if that's what you mean."

"No. I mean, like, can you feel its energy?"

She smiles wide like a thousand stars lighting up her face.

She has July in her eyes, I think. But I don't think it. I hear it. On the inside of me, but not my head voice.

I want to go over and touch the knife too. To feel what is making Ronnie squeal with delight, but the basement door opens, and Barbara descends the stairs.

She glides majestically into the musty basement, wrapped in a flowing red silk robe. The bottom of it trails behind her like a bride's dress on her wedding day. Elegant. Magnificent. Enchanting. Her dark hair is tied tightly in a bun at the top of her head, and there is not a speck of makeup on her pale skin. She is all flesh. Pure and cleansed. And as she walks into the center of the room where we are, the lightbulb flickers like it's winking at her. Bowing to her. Like it's straining to match her luminous presence.

Barbara.

To even think the letters of her name stirs something wicked and wild in me. And as she makes her way to the circle (the circle that *I* drew for her) and lets the robe languidly fall from her shoulders, I stand in awe of her in her full, naked glory. Ancient symbols adorn her body from neck to foot. Meticulously drawn onto her skin in either paint or maybe even blood, I can't be sure. I don't know what they are, but they are a series of harsh lines. Runes, I think. They cover the entirety of her, like looking at an ancient and forbidden book. The tattooed lady who casts a spell on the world.

Quickly, Ronnie rushes over, swoops up the garment and places it on the workbench. Barbara saunters around the circle, and my heart kinda flutters with excitement as she inspects the markings on the floor. She gives me a quick nod of approval, and I swell. Donna bucks against the restraints in the chair and tries harder and harder to free her face from the gag.

"Should I sedate her again?" Ronnie asks.

Barbara watches intently as Donna struggles in place. "No. No," she says waving her hand in the air. She walks over and kneels down before her, looking at her with awe. She stares deeply into her eyes, and Donna seems to calm down a bit. "You are made of water," Barbara whispers to her. "You flow so easily."

Donna's eyes flash for a second—they flash with horror and fear then suddenly go into a hazy daze, like she had taken the biggest, longest, deepest bong hit. She stares into space, but the space is Barbara's eyes. Her shoulders relax and slump forward, and she no longer fights to get free.

"I am made of fire," Barbara continues. "I burn brightly." And there in Donna's eyes, I see from across the room, a red flame flare up in her vacant reflection.

Donna makes a soft moan.

"Untie her," Barbara says to Ronnie.

"What?" Ronnie answers. "But she's…"

"Untie her," she repeats, more sternly this time. "She'll be a good girl. Won't you, sweet pea? She knows she'll get burned if she tries to move."

Ronnie goes behind her and unties the restraints. Donna quickly brings her hand to her face, pulls the cloth gag down, and opens her mouth as if to let out the loudest scream possible.

Barbara wags her long forefinger in front of Donna's face. "Uh-uh-uh. That's not how we act." And she places Donna's hands in her lap, laying her own on top of them. "Trixie, bring me the athame."

Excitedly, I fetch the knife and feel the girth of it immediately. Just like Ronnie said. It's a hefty tool, but there's something more to it than just its weight. The metal of it *sings*. Sings in my head. Hums in my blood. Echoes in my stomach. A choir. A chorus. Angels in heaven. It's that song again, and it makes my veins throb. Pulse. My head fills with the song. My ears fill with the song. And it all stops in an instant when I hand the tool over to Barbara.

Barbara runs the blade up and down the outside of Donna's folded palms, not hard enough to draw blood, but rough enough to leave little scratch marks. Poor Donna squirms instinctively. "It won't hurt you if you let me," Barbara says.

"Please," Donna pleads. "Just let me go. I'll do whatever you want, but just let me go. I just want to go home." A harrowing sob constricts her chest, and she has trouble catching her breath.

"Easy, easy," Barbara coaxes as she opens one of Donna's palms and makes a slice in her thumb with the knife.

Donna yelps in pain.

"It's because she's not one of us," Ronnie whispers to me from the side of her mouth. I nod even though I'm not entirely sure what she meant. She mumbles something else, but I don't pay her any mind and keep my attention on Barbara who has taken Donna's finger into her mouth.

"Close enough," she says breathlessly, happily, after taking her fill of her blood.

"Are you sure?" Ronnie asks. "You said you were sure about the last one, too."

Barbara throws an angry look her way. "I'm sure *now*," she says.

"Sure about what? What are you talking about? What do you mean? Who are you people? What are you doing to me? Please, just let me go home! I just want to go home!" Donna's frantic pleas bring Barbara to her feet. Her heavy breasts bobble up and down as she moves. Putting a forefinger under Donna's chin, she tilts her head to look up at her, and when Donna's eyes meet Barbara's, Donna goes still again—relaxed, subdued, entranced. Barbara speaks directly into her mind, and I am jealous that I can't hear the words. I need to hear what Barbara is saying! I need to know the exact words that put Donna into such a hypnotic state. I want to be in Barbara's inner circle and know all the Coven's secrets!

Ronnie goes behind Donna again and brings her arms above her head. With the knife, Barbara goes underneath Donna's sweater and slices it up the middle, and Ronnie pulls it off and tosses it to the floor. Donna's breasts bounce freely in their place. Round and supple, yet firm and hard. Her skin is soft and white—not quite as pale as Barbara's—a more cream color, milky. Her peach-colored nipples stand at attention like two sentries on duty, and something about her rack delights me, makes me raise an eyebrow. Ronnie, too, likes what she sees. She's practically salivating over her, and she works feverishly to unbutton her jeans and peel them off her! Donna's jeans and panties fall to the floor, and she sits naked as the tears of both horror and shame overcome her.

I stir again, like lightning flashing between my legs, and it makes me think this intense attraction to naked Donna is suspect. There's a smell in the air, and it's not just the dampness of the basement or the remnants of past rituals on the concrete. There's the scent of iron in the atmosphere. Metallic. Sour almost. It's a mixture of fear and desire and primordial instinct.

And womanhood.

Suddenly, it dawns on me that Donna is approaching her moontime! That must be why Barbara got giddy when she tasted her blood. It makes sense now that not only does the ritual have to be timed correctly, but the subject must be at the right *time*.

Without being asked, and without hesitation, I pick up the clothes and take them over to the workbench where Barbara's robe is. Something tells me that nothing can be inside the circle.

Except Barbara.

She hands the athame to Ronnie and a twinge of jealousy twists in my stomach (*why didn't she give it to me?*) and lies down in the center of the circle. She hums, a low growl in her chest, and she breathes in deeply every time the tune changes. When her breasts heave up and down, the writing on her skin gives a soft, subtle glow, or that could just be my eyes adjusting to the basement light. But I don't think so. My eyesight has been changed. No, what I see truly is Barbara glowing!

"Because I am the truth, and the light, and the way, Trixie," she says to me through a big, knowing smile. Her eyes are closed, and she places her arms at her sides. I wish I could read what her body says—her beautifully shaped body with glowing paint markings all over.

"Yes, ma'am," I respond.

"You are the Earth, Trixie. Ronnie is the air. With you by my side, we will combine water with fire. Do you understand what I ask of you?"

I nod even though I don't.

"Are you willing to accept the sacrifice at your hands for the praise and glory of their names?"

What she says doesn't make sense, but somehow it does. "Yes," Ronnie mutters.

"Yes," I repeat.

"Pray, my sisters, that this blood sacrifice may be acceptable to the old ones. Let us begin."

Ronnie looks at me and raises her eyebrows. "You ready?"

My hands are slick with anxiety. Nerves. Fear. "Ready for what?"

"To bring back Barbara's children. The Blood Sister and Blood Brother."

Donna's head rolls to the side of her neck like a limp baby doll.

"Yes," I say with fake confidence, because really, I'm practically pissing myself right about now. Ronnie waves the athame in the air, beckoning me to come over. "Hold her arms up in the air," she instructs, and I obey.

"Forced bleeding of the New Moon," Barbara says, but it doesn't sound like Barbara. It sounds like multiple voices all at once. Like a chorus of distorted sounds echoing in the room.

Ronnie spreads Donna's legs apart exposing the flowery lips of her sex. Perfect and pink, I look over Donna's shoulder to catch a glimpse of what has gotten us all worked up. It's definitely a glorious sight in the dim light. But my eyes can see! I can see her outer lips glisten with anticipation and radiate with shame. She likes this violation, but she hates that she likes it, and therein lies her guilt—her agonizing humiliation. She tilts her head back to look at me. Her blue eyes beg me to help her, and as she tries to get the words out, she has no voice. Barbara has taken it away from her. There are no sounds from her throat, just lips moving frantically. "Help me. Help me," she says in her silence. All I can do is stare at her frantic eyes when she realizes she cannot speak.

Ronnie moves the athame seductively up the inside of Donna's leg leaving a trail of goose-bumps in its wake. She gently teases the flesh of her nether lips with the metal, prying them apart, letting the juices coat the little area of the pointed tip. Donna's body tenses up in confusion. Her mind and body at war with itself over fulfilling a desire and her impending death. With my free hand, I push her hair back from her forehead, smoothing it down her back and giving her a little "shhh" to help calm her down. She relaxes for a second, but then Ronnie plunges the knife into Donna's sex, and pumps it in and out of her a few times. "The maiden's blood," she says.

Donna's eyes go wide—wider than I've ever seen a person's eyes before—and her mouth opens in a terrifying, silent scream. She feels all the pain. The burning sensation of her flesh ripped open, the heat of the blood now pouring from between her legs. And she's screaming—screaming on the inside because her voice is now lost to the ether. Her voice is now lost in the gaping void of the heavens, in that place I saw when I tasted Barbara's blood, that place with all the stars that have all the crazy names.

Ronnie takes the knife out from her and runs it up the length of her stomach, up to the center of her chest, then drags the blade on the underside of both her breasts. Not just a light line, though, it's more of a deep and hard gouging of Donna's flesh. A thick, ropey line oozing red. Jagged and frayed edges of skin torn apart at the seams. Donna's shoulders go limp, and her eyes close shut as she passes out from the pain. "The mother's milk," Ronnie says.

She drops the athame into the circle next to Barbara and joins me. Together we lift Donna from the chair as Barbara opens her legs. "Bring her here! Now!" she exclaims as she writhes her hips passionately on the floor. Ronnie and I lay Donna on top of Barbara. She wraps her legs around Donna's waist, grips her backside, and grinds herself against the bloody mass of flesh.

Donna's blood coats every inch of Barbara's skin. It blends with the painted symbols until they are no longer visible, and their bodies are just forms of sticky red. Barbara lets out an ecstatic cry, picks up the athame next to her. "Accept this sacrifice," she says. "Let them be the word made flesh," and she plunges the blade into the side of Donna's neck. Blood hisses out like steam coming up from a hot skillet, and Donna's lifeless body goes limp in Barbara's embrace.

Chapter Twelve

Sunday, May 2nd 1965
Barbara Thorne's House
163 North Shelby Avenue
Salem, Illinois
Morning of the Waxing Crescent Moon

I struggle with trying to process everything that has been happening. I feel as if I'm in some kind of fever-dream nightmare, and I can't escape. But do I want to escape is the real question. I don't know. I feel like I'm drunk all the time. Or high. Like I've smoked grass from the moment my eyes open up in the morning to the moment I close them to sleep. And the feeling doesn't stop even in my sleep—my dreams are fever-like and filled with hallucinatory images and sounds. Like I'm on LSD or something. *But I'm not.*

Maybe Cyrinda is right—maybe there is something in this house that is changing me, shifting my perceptions, making me feel and think and do things that are completely alien to me. She left the house yesterday afternoon, right after our argument. Mumbled something about going to

Julius to get my job at the movie theatre, and how she was gonna "show me." I assume he started training her—I mean, with June missing, and me quitting, he still needs to run his business, and Cyrinda is pretty enough for the role, so… She never came home last night, which was good because she wasn't here for the ceremony. In fact, she's still not home. Curious. It's not like Cyrinda to stay out all night. Maybe she met up with Clark and Kent and…

The morning breeze whips through my hair, and I pump my legs out and in on the swing in the backyard. It's a rickety old thing that practically comes up out of the ground the higher I go, but I don't care. It feels good to fly in the air for a few seconds at a time—to be lifted in the sky when the weight of the world is desperately trying to bring me back down to the gravity laden earth. When I was a kid, when I was small and alone and afraid, I took solace in the freedom of the swing. I would try to go as high as I possibly could. To run. To escape. To fly away up to the clouds where no one could find me. Or yell at me. Or hit me. Foster moms with shrill voices pierced my ears and shook me to my guts. Foster dads with heavy hands too quick to strike for the most minor offenses. When I cried myself to sleep at night, I always remembered to be thankful for the torments I *didn't* receive. It could have been worse—much worse—but innocence is a layered onion, and even though I had plenty of sections intact, there were far too many peels that were already unfurled.

Run. Escape. Fly away.

The three things I had longed to do, I ended up accomplishing.

Run. I ran from it all. Exactly one month ago, I ran from the harsh voices and quick striking hands.

Escape. I escaped my never-ending, day-to-day torture with my best friend by my side.

Fly away. I flew the night I drank the blood of my hostess. Barbara. Sweet Barbara. My mysterious protector. She took me in, welcomed me into her home, made me a part of something important. She believes in me. She trusts me. I can't let her down. I know she needs me for her project. But just what her project is, I'm not entirely sure about. I know she has powers, I mean, it's so obvious that she's some kind of other-worldly being, my very own Samantha, and I know she wants to like, maybe raise her kids from the dead? I don't know. It's jumbled and confusing and only makes sense for a fleeting moment in my head, but when I try to fit all the pieces together, it really doesn't. So, here's what I do know—Barbara protected me and sheltered me more than any other so-called mother I have ever lived with. I want to make her proud. I want to please her. And I know that blood is important. There is blood all over this house—metaphorically and literally.

What ends up happening to Donna is not for me to know. Or so said Ronnie. After Barbara's ritual, Ronnie told me to go upstairs and take a shower and get some rest. So, I listened, only the "rest" part was an impossibility. My mind raced a thousand miles a minute with all the whys and what-ifs and hows. *How* were they going to clean up all that blood? *How* were they going to get rid of Donna's body? *How* were they going to conceal everything? *What if* that had been me—an unsuspecting runaway fallen prey to their ritual? *Why* Donna? *Why* this night? *How* was the ritual supposed to work anyway?

"Easy," Barbara had coaxed, smiling at me. Her face and body was a cracked mask of dried red. She ran her fingers through the side of my head and whispered, "Just keep your good thoughts flowing, Trixie, for you are the truth and the light and the way sent to me on the wings of the locust. I could never harm you. Ronnie and I will handle everything. Don't fret, my pet."

And somehow, that's all it took to put me at ease, but now with the sun already risen and no sign of Cyrinda anywhere to be found, my nerves and suspicions start to get the best of me. A sinking feeling invades my stomach as a terrifying thought forms in my mind and nearly paralyzes me: *They must have found her!* I think I actually say the words out loud in my distressed state. The cops, detectives, investigators—whoever—must have found her at the movie theatre last night, taken her in for questioning, and are getting ready to come get me at Barbara's any second! There's no other explanation! Shy little, meek little, Nervous Nelly, Scary Mary Cyrinda probably spilled the beans about where we are and what we're doing. What *am I* doing? They'll be here in no time, I surmise! They'll be here and insist I go back to Indianapolis because technically, we're still minors. Geez Louise! Cyrinda is probably halfway back there for all I know.

I tuck my legs in and grind my feet into the dirt stopping the force of the swing. I jerk back and forth a few times before I get my footing and quickly hop off as the thick plastic seat grazes the backs of my thighs violently like it's giving me a forceful push to get the hell out of there! I race back into the house, snatch June's missing flyer off my nightstand, and trot to the kitchen to call Clark. If the cops are coming for me, I sure as hell ain't gonna be here when they show.

Clark seems surprised when he realizes it's me on the line. His voice shifts, and I can hear a smile form on his face on the other end of the line. Did he not think I was going to call? Did he not think I would want to help put up flyers for June? I mean, regardless of my current intent, I hope June will be found.

Even though I know she won't be.

"When do you want to go?" he asks, cheerily.

"Um, I guess as soon as possible. Now is good for me." I try not to sound too anxious, but honestly, the anxiety is strangling me from the inside out. I need to run. Escape. Fly. And that needs to happen now.

"Oh, um, yeah?" he stammers, and my stomach flops. If he pulls out some crap about needing to get ready, I think I will scream.

I pause. "Yeah, why? No good?"

"No, no, no!" he answers quickly. "Now's good. I can be there in say… ten?"

"Hurry," I say, and my mouth pops shut with embarrassment. Now he's going to think I'm desperate to see him or something when in reality I am just super anxious to leave.

Curiously, I hear his smile widen again. "I'll do my best." And he hangs up the phone.

I frankly don't give a shit that I'm wearing one of Ronnie's old button-down shirts and a pair of faded dungarees. I frankly don't give a shit that I don't have any makeup on or that my hair is a rat's nest. What I do give a shit about is the dried blood still under my fingernails from last night, and that the scent of iron is still up my nose. I wonder if Clark will be able to smell the metallic odor on me, or if it's just embedded in my nostrils. That's definitely not a chance I want to take, so I try scrubbing the last remnants of dried blood and use some of Barbara's patchouli oil on my neck and wrists and behind my ears. The fragrance is a success… the scrubbing, not so much. Or is it just something I can see? Am I making a bigger deal out of this than it is? Frantically, I search the bathroom's medicine cabinet for some nail polish to hide the stain. To hide the sin. But before I can do a quick cover-up job, the car horn honks. I jolt on the inside from the shock of it, then sigh with relief knowing I have at least a few more hours to evade the police.

"That's an interesting smell," he remarks when I get in and close the door, and my heart all but freezes in my chest. Does he smell the blood smell? The death smell? Poor Donna's gutted vagina smell?

I gulp. It's clearly audible because Clark smirks.

"You steal someone's perfume?" he chides as he pulls away from the house.

I force a little laugh. "Sorta. Ronnie's patchouli oil."

"Total hippy shit," he huffs, and his eyes do a semi-roll.

"Totally," I agree as I relax my shoulders.

"You don't strike me as the hippy type."

"I'm not."

"That's the way June would smell every time she came back from one of those meetings. Like they doused her in it."

I pick up the stack of flyers in between us and pound them against the leather so they're stacked neatly.

"June didn't like them," he continues. "She did at first, but said things got real weird real fast."

"I don't mind them," I say, feeling the need to defend Barbara and Ronnie.

"Hippies," he grumbles.

"Nah," I say, trying to downplay it, "they're totally harmless. Barbara took us in. Strangers. That was a big risk for her. She didn't have to do that."

"Hippy bullshit commune crap. Did she take in that girl who was with you, too? The one who was with you at the bus stop?"

My back stiffens, and I feel the blood drain from my face. I pray to God he doesn't notice—that he's so concentrated on the road to notice the very obvious quick shift in my demeanor. Ignoring his comment, I keep my focus on the flyers as he makes a left onto Boone Street. "So, why are we going to Centralia?"

"How did you know we were going to Centralia?" he asks, alarmed.

"Um, you mentioned it when I saw you yesterday."

"Oh yeah, yeah, right. Centralia. Well, June used to go to some youth group over there when we were in junior high. If she really did run away, she might have gone there, and someone might have seen her."

"Wouldn't they have already checked there, though? I mean, Centralia is kinda close to Salem, and June's mom and the police seem to have been all over the place and..."

"I don't know, Trixie," he says, exasperated. "I just feel like I gotta keep trying. Something. Anything."

"No, no, no!" I say in agreement. "I totally understand. Cover all the bases. Let's bring Junebug home."

He smiles at me but keeps his eyes on the road. My insides flop around again because somehow I know that's not going to happen. Somehow

I know June is somewhere over the rainbow. Maybe in the Land of Oz. Somehow I know it was her bloodstains on the basement floor mixed with oil and paint and other bodily fluids. She's with Donna and who knows how many countless others there have been or will be. But I could never say that to Clark, so off to Centralia we go. Besides, I have a tail to lose.

"Hey, Clark?" I ask after some silence.

"Mmmm hmmm," he mutters.

"Did my friend come to the movie theatre yesterday afternoon?"

"Who, Ronnie?" he asks.

"No, my other friend. Cyrinda. She hung out with us once when I first started working with you guys. Super cute. Super shy. Kinda a wallflower."

His face screws up to the side. "Cyrinda?"

"Yeah. My best friend. She and I came out here together, and…"

"I know you're a runaway. You don't have to pretend anymore," he says bluntly, cutting me off.

I swallow hard. "How did you…?"

"I'm not stupid, and it's kinda obvious. That Barbara lady is known to help girls like you."

"And Cyrinda."

"Hmmm," he grunts.

"I swear, Clark, I had zero to do with June's disappearance, if that's what you're implying!" I shout defensively.

"Wait. What? What do you mean? I never said anything like that," he says calmly.

"You didn't have to. It's your tone of voice. Like, you're accusing me of something. But I swear to God, I did not influence her in any way to run. We never even talked about it. I thought everything with her was hunky dory. And she didn't even know I was a runaway."

"She did," he says matter-of-factly. "It was pretty damn obvious."

"Oh," I say, and my body goes cold.

"Look, you did what you had to do. Whatever the rhyme or reason for it, no one judged you. We all liked you from the start. You're a pretty cool chick. I don't really care about any of that."

"You don't?" I squeak with a hint of disbelief in my voice.

"Nah. Small fries," he says dismissively with a grin.

I can't help but smile back at him. I feel a little more relaxed. A little less guarded. My smile stays plastered on my face from ear to ear. All goofy and stuff, like I'm some kinda crazy person in a looney bin. Clark's crystal blue eyes make my insides warm and tingly, and I'm so nervous that I can't stop fidgeting with the flyers in my lap. He notices my movements and takes one hand off the wheel and puts in on top of my knee. A gush of warmth rushes between my legs, and boy-oh-oh, are those butterflies in my tummy going wild! I don't move his hand away. In fact, I place one of mine on top of his as if to secure it in place. I press it firmly against my knee holding him there, silently telling him not to let go.

We ride the whole way to Centralia. Highway 51 takes us right into the heart of the city. When he turns off the main road, I ask him where we're going.

"Foundation Park," he says. "It's a pretty nice place, and a lot of kids our age hang out there. I figure it's our best bet to actually speak to someone who may have seen June."

"Makes sense," I say and look longingly out the window. The greenery is in full bloom this early May, and I am enthralled with all the pretty colors of the park.

Clark pulls the car over and points out the passenger side window. "See out there?" he says, and I follow the line of his hand to a small structure in the middle of an open clearing.

"Yuh huh," I respond. "What about it?"

"That's The Miner's Memorial Shelter. Like I said, it's kinda become a hangout spot over the years, so June's flyer should get lots of visibility. That place is a memorial site dedicated to the miners who lost their lives in a freak accident back in '47."

"Oh geez! That's kinda awful."

"One hundred eleven people died that day. My grandfather was one of them."

I gasp. "That's not *kinda* awful—that *is* awful. I'm so sorry!"

"Yeah," he says pensively, "they say Centralia is cursed. That's why my family moved to Salem after the accident. Did you know that there's a city in Pennsylvania called Centralia? And *they* had a mining accident a few years back?"

"Are you serious, Clark?"

"Scouts honor. That accident caused a seam fire that still burns to this day. Left the place a ghost town."

"Wow," I say, but there's a hint of confusion in my voice because I'm not quite making the connection to what he's saying to me. "I never knew that."

"They say Salem is cursed too. All of them. All of them witches put some kind of spell on any town that has that name."

"Oh stop!" I say and swat his shoulder. "You don't believe in that, do you?"

"Witches? Nah. Maybe not. Curses? Definitely yes."

"What makes you say that?"

"Just weird stuff happens in these places. Constantly."

"Like June."

"Like June," he repeats woefully. "And others."

"People don't just vanish, ya know," I say, but I'm not sure if I'm trying to convince him or myself.

"Well, you haven't been paying attention, have you," he bites.

I roll my eyes and huff. "You know what I mean."

"I know," he mumbles.

"Be honnest with me," I say. "Where do you think June really is?"

He sighs deeply. "I honestly don't know. She used to tell me about her favorite place in the world—Cape Girardeau in Missouri. She used to go there in the summer with her family."

Hearing the name of the city makes my stomach flutter. It's an odd sensation that both frightens and delights me at the same time. My interest is piqued. "Missouri?"

"Right on the Mississippi River. About two and a half hours from here."

"So why haven't you gone there yet?" I ask.

He runs his hand through his dark brown hair and his eyes go dark with sadness. "I don't know, maybe because there's a part of me that's in denial."

"Denial about what?" I pry, but I already know what he's going to say because I feel the same way too. As a matter of fact, I'm almost certain June is…

"Dead," he says outright. His lack of emotion behind the word jars me, takes me aback. "I feel like she's dead."

I clutch the tops of the flyers in my lap. "Don't talk like that," I try to say with a comforting voice. "We can't give up hope. C'mon, let's go put up these flyers in the Miner's Shelter."

He gives me a small smile and turns his body to fully face me. "You're right," he says, and he puts his hand back on my knee. "I'm just glad that you called."

"What do you mean? Why wouldn't I have?"

"Well, we just started to hang out, and then everything happened with June, and then you quit…" his voice trails off a bit. "You're really a groovy chick, and I was hoping to get to know you better. I don't know. I was kinda bummed that we didn't have a chance to have more time together, so this is really nice."

My cheeks flush red like two hot pokers seared the sides of my face. But I don't care that he sees me blushing. I want him to see me blush.

"Yes. This *is* nice," I say with my chin cocked down against my chest. Only my eyes peer up at him, staring deeply into the abyss of his. They have gone from crystal blue to jet black, as his pupils have dilated across the entire circumference of his eyeball.

Slowly, he reaches his hand up under my chin, and with his forefinger, he lifts my face to meet his. His mouth descends upon mine and our lips engage in a sweet and gentle kiss. One peck, two pecks, then he opens his mouth wider, and my rhythm matches his. Open. Shut. Open shut. Before I know it, he darts his tongue into my mouth and invites mine to dance with his. Back and forth our heads sway as our tongues move more feverishly, more frantically. My breathing heightens to short, quick, passionate pants as he moves closer to me and slips one hand under my shirt. My skin blooms with goosebumps when his fingers make contact and inch slowly up to my chest. He fumbles a little getting underneath the fabric of my bra, but I exhale in delight when he cups one of my breasts in his hand and rolls the fleshy nub of my nipple between his fingers, and the flyers scatter all over the car floor.

His mouth releases from mine, and he moves closer still, kissing my cheek and my ear then working his way down my neck. He places his free hand in between my legs and furiously rubs my crotch. The tickling sensation even through the thick denim makes me squirm.

"You're so beautiful," he breathes heavily into my ear. "You're so warm and filled with light."

Breaking me from the swoon of his touch and his lips on my flesh and his hot breath like warm honey coating my neck, Barbara's voice comes bounding in my head. Her voice is so loud and so clear that I can't ignore it or the pressure above my eyes that comes with it: *So now, with you here with me, I can protect that light—we can protect that light. Keep it pure. Keep it safe.* Her words pierce through me, like a shockwave down my spine, and I realize that I can't let Clark go any further. If I lie down in the backseat of his car and let him have his way with me, my light will be extinguished forever. And then what good would I be to Barabara? She would have no use for me. No need for me. I would play no role in her mission, nor would I have a position in the Crimson Coven. Would I end up like Donna? *Or June?* I shudder to think...

I pull back from Clark—squirm uncomfortably about an inch away from his touch. He stops and looks up at me puzzled. "What's wrong? What's the matter?"

"I... I... I just can't," I stammer. "I mean... I... I want to. And this is so very nice, but..."

He recoils and puts his hands in the air like a criminal in surrender. "Oh," he says curtly. "Say no more. Say. No. More."

Nervously, I try to scoop up the flyers from the floor. "Please," I practically beg. "I really want to be here with you. I mean... I really want to go with you. I just... I just..."

"It's fine," he says, but there is zero effect in his voice. "It's groovy, Mama. A-okay. We should probably go put up those flyers anyway and head back home."

"Yeah. Sure," I agree, but my chest feels hollow with shame and guilt, and the ache between my legs throbs painfully with absent desire.

Chapter Thirteen

Monday, May 3rd 1965
Eastlawn Cemetery
North Shelby Avenue
Salem, Illinois
Early Morning of the Waxing Crescent Moon

Clark and I barely spoke to each other on the drive back from Centralia. It was definitely a different feeling from when he picked me up and practically drove the whole way there with his hand on my knee. The ride back was cold. Quiet. Uncomfortable. I messed up royally with him, and I knew it. It made me shudder on the inside.

I fiddled with the radio a few times on the way home, but there was nothing but talking and commercials and some cowboy music. Right as we turned onto North Shelby, "Me and My Shadow" came on the radio. I tensed up, and I quickly turned the dial to shut it off.

"Hey!" Clark howled. "I like that song."

"Oh, I can't stand Bing Crosby," I lied. "Too old-fashioned for my taste."

He turned the radio back on. "Understandable. But a little Bing never hurt nobody!"

That was the most enthusiastic he had spoken to me in almost an hour. Like, the real Clark that I knew was coming back out again. Or maybe the silent-treatment Clark was the real Clark, and the jokey, jovial Clark was the Clark who was only trying to get into my pants. I don't know. All I know is I was feeling kinda awful and blue and my heart kinda ached in a weird way, and I couldn't pinpoint why.

Bing Crosby crooned, "And when it's twelve o'clock, we climb the stairs. And we never knock, for there's nobody there."

Cyrinda's face suddenly flashed in my mind. Frantically, I asked Clark what time it was. He looked down at his watch and chuckled. "Oh, wouldn't you know? Twelve o'clock. What a coinkidink!"

Thankfully, we were close to the house and when Clark pulled over and came to a stop, he said, "Back to the house of horrors!" with a laugh.

I don't know what was written on my face, but I felt my ears get hot. I was partially angry for him putting down Barbara, and partially scared that he knew something. 'Cause, yeah, some pretty horrific things had happened in that house. *Probably even to June.*

"You know, June told me that Ronnie chick tried to kiss her once. And that the Barbara lady tried to get her to join some kind of coven. The Red Coven? The Blood Coven?"

"Crimson," I blurted.

"Yeah, yeah, crimson. So fucking weird."

"It's not all that bad," I said, trying to convince him. Or maybe myself. Either way, my voice was pretty stern and indignant.

He sighed. "Sure, Darlin'. Whatever floats your boat."

I had barely stepped my feet out and shut the door before he was vrooming away.

Stupid jerk. Stupid boy. Left me standing in the middle of the street. A proper gentleman would at least wait until I got safely inside the house. But now I stand here wondering: If only he *did* know the truth. If only I had the moxie to tell him.

Clark's taillights are no longer visible, and I turn on my heel to race into the house. My thoughts shift to Cyrinda, and that pit in my stomach returns. She had been so far from my thoughts today that I am wracked to my throat with guilt. I pray she's inside at the kitchen table drinking some hot chocolate and listening to Barbara and Ronnie jibber jabber about something or other. Or maybe she's in bed snuggled up under the covers waiting for me to come home.

Suddenly, something from across the street catches the corner of my eye, and I stop and turn my head toward the cemetery. Something flickered. Moved. *Waved.* Yet there was no breeze, and there's no one out here on the dark street except me. The streetlamp flickers, and for some reason, my breath catches in my throat. I stare hard across the rows of headstones, trying to look far down deep into the cemetery.

Nothing.

Nothing.

And some more nothing.

Until a shadow manifests from behind the trees and up from the headstones like a looming presence in the den of death. It takes everything in me to keep from screaming and running, but much like voiceless Donna, the sound doesn't come out. My legs don't seem to work.

…and we never knock for there's nobody there.

"Cyrinda?" I call out in a hushed tone. I don't know why, though. Call it a feeling or something.

"All alone and feeling blue," she responds and within seconds, she comes into full view.

I take off at a sprint across the street, through the rows of the dead, and meet her by a large oak tree. I throw my arms around her neck and pull down on her into a violent swing. "What in God's green-apple Earth are you doing out here? Where have you been? You never came home! Everyone was worried sick about you!"

"Oh. Really?" she asks blandly as she arches her eyebrow.

"*I* was worried sick. That's all that matters." I say releasing my hold on her. I take a step back and sweep her blonde bangs away from her eyes.

"I hate when we don't get along," she whimpers in a soft voice.

"You think *I* like it?" I squawk.

She gives a little giggle. "No. I know."

"So, what the hell happened? Where did you go? Where have you been?" I urge.

Suddenly I notice something in Cyrinda's demeanor seems different. Changed. She rolls her head as if to look at the entirety of the cemetery.

"Here?" I yell. "In the cemetery? All this time?"

She nods. "I needed to clear my head. To think. To process."

"All this time?" I repeat.

"Yes. I guess I just lost track."

"What about Julius? I thought you were going to try to get a job over at the movie theatre?"

"Oh, fuck the movie theatre, Trixie!"

"Cyrinda!" I reprimand.

"Look, I've done a lot of thinking out here. Can't we just agree that we were both right?"

"Right about what?"

"I was right that this place is changing you. You were right that I haven't been much of a helpful friend lately. We're in this together. We started this together. We'll see it through together. I know you have some kind of thing that you're doing with Ronnie and Barbara. That's fine. I'm not a part of it. I accepted that, and I will respect that. But please, promise me, once that's over— promise me we'll leave here. Together."

I extend my arms out and reach for hers. She interlocks her fingers in mine, and I sigh. "I know it seems like I'm losing the plot, but I promise, it'll all come together. And when it does, when it's over, we'll talk about what we're gonna do next. Just please, for Pete's sake, don't ask me to go back to Indianapolis."

She nods her head and releases her hands from my grip. "I'm going back to the house," she says. "I'm pretty tired."

I look up at the sky and the clouds shift across the face of the moon. From behind the darkness of them, a silver sliver peeks out and smiles at me. *I know you,* I say to her on the inside, and I remember the night I felt like I flew in the sky. I touched the moon that night. I was filled with powerful blood to do powerful things and see powerful sights. Poor June. Maybe if she had accepted Barbara's gift of sistership, she'd be here in the cemetery with me right now. "Go," I say to Cyrinda. "I'll be in in a bit."

"Don't stay out too late," she calls over her shoulder.

"Don't worry," I say laughing. "My name's not Cyrinda!"

Her laughter echoes in the street. I hold on to the sound of it in my head until it fades away and is replaced by other sounds—night sounds, cemetery sounds, tree branch rustling sounds, wind moaning sounds, children laughing in the distance sounds, music sounds. I pause and home in on the song that plays in the night sky—the song for the thin smile of the moon, the song for me. It energizes me when the sound reaches my ears. Makes me want to dance. It takes me back to that special night in the den when I was made a member of the coven. I close my eyes and sway.

This is my song, I think. *The witches sing it for me and me alone.*

But my solo dance is interrupted by the sound of children's laughter. Remnants of Cyrinda's voice transformed. It was there before, but faint like background noise on the wind. But this time, it's loud and startling and snaps me to attention. "Not for you," a child's voice says.

"Is somebody there?" I call out, but only the wind forces the sound of my voice back to my ears.

After a second or two of dead silence, the laughter grows amidst the trees again, like it moves. Like it runs. The sound travels together then splits apart by the oak tree and goes off in opposite directions, so it feels like it's in stereo. And it's not just in my head. It's all around me. Surrounding me. The laughter of two children. The presence of two children. The unseen.

"The unborn," a voice whispers, but it's right at my neck—a voice, a breath, up against my ear, breathing, sighing heavily then rushing away. I scream, and as my body jolts, another fit of laughter pierces the night.

"Who's there?" I call out, my voice barely making it out of my throat.

"Shhh," one of the voices says. "You'll wake it up." It's a girl's voice.

"Abomination," says the other who sounds like a boy.

"Spawn of Satan," the girl's voice taunts, and they both go into a laughing frenzy again. Their voices are wavy, shaky, like crackles over a bad phone connection, but underneath the drumming music of the moon, I can hear them perfectly.

"Who's there?" This time I yell forcefully.

"Let them be cleansed," the girl whispers. I get the feeling that they're not speaking directly to me, or at me, but *for* me. Like they have a message for me.

"David? Gretchen?" I say out to the sky. Is it possible that I am in the presence of Barbara's children? Are they reaching across space and time to bring me a message? Am I to be the catalyst to bring them back to life? Do they see my light, too?

"…the light and the way," the girl says, but her words are cut off. Only sounds coming in sputters.

They laugh again.

"Let them all suffer," the boy's voice says, but his is barely coming through too.

"Let who suffer?" I ask.

"Infection," the girl's voice says, and I fear the weakness of the sound means they're fading away.

"What are you trying to tell me? I don't understand."

"Blood…"

"…hek…," they say simultaneously.

"Bloodheksa? Barbara? Your mother? Is that what you mean?"

"Blood…"

"…innocent…"

"…only way."

"Cape…"

"Slow down, slow down! I don't understand!"

"Child…"

"…sacrifice…"

"Child sacrifice?" I ask. "What do you mean?"

"Only way."

"Only way."

"Deal with you…"

"…later."

"Innocent blood."

"Innocent blood."

"Blodheksa."

"Blodheksa."

"The house…"

"…the house."

"The house…"

"…of Arrah."

"Arrah? The witch, Arrah? What about her?" I say.

They laugh again, but they are barely audible. Eventually, their voices disintegrate into the ether. The music stops and the clouds cover up the smiling moon, and I am left alone once more in the cemetery. No longer do I feel their presence or hear their voices. My mind tries desperately to remember the words I heard. I know I'll have to run back into the house and write it all down before I forget them. I know I will spend count-less moments analyzing what the "child sacrifice" is. I wish they could have explained themselves to me instead of leaving me with these rid-dles. And they're not really riddles either. Just fragments of conversations pushed down from the great beyond.

The arms of the oak tree sway in the breeze, and a cold wind pierces me to the bone. It's a chill that needles its way underneath my skin and settles down deep. My foster mother used to say that if you ever got so cold that you couldn't warm yourself up right away, that's when you knew the devil got ya. The devil likes cold places 'cause he has lots of opportunities to make them hot. I scoff at the memory of the old wives' tale, but for some reason, I can't shake some deep-rooted sense of fear deep inside me. I hurriedly trot back across the street to the house and rush inside the front door.

When she hears the door open, Barbara comes out from the kitchen to meet me in the foyer. Her long brown hair is pinned up in a perfect messy bun. Her white blouse is untucked from her bell-bottom jeans, but I can still get a sense of her voluptuous body underneath the baggy shirt. I blink rapidly when I see her because all I can think about is her naked flesh covered in black markings mixed with blood.

Donna's dead, I absentmindedly think to myself. *Donna's dead, and I think I killed her.*

"It's okay," Barbara says, and a part of me knows she's validating my internal thoughts. A look of concern sweeps over her face, darkening her soft brown eyes. "Where were you?" she inquires.

I give a soft chuckle because I feel like I just had the same conversation with Cyrinda, and I think: *Gee, communication around here is pretty lackluster.*

"I went to Centralia with Clark today so we could hang up June's missing posters."

Barbara raises her eyebrows suspiciously, and I notice there are no lines on her forehead. No wrinkles. I know she's not old, but even *my* forehead crinkles up when I frown or smile or make any facial gesture for that matter. *Must be all that young female blood she bathes in...*

"Annnndd?" she drawls.

I shake my head with quick movements. "And what?" I ask, confused.

"Did anything happen?" she asks. "You know. *Between* the two of you?"

"Oh!" I answer when I realize what she's implying. "No! Nothing like that!"

She breathes a sigh of relief. "Excellent. So, what's wrong? You look like you've seen a ghost."

I pause and inhale sharply. "Well..." I begin.

My hesitation piques her interest, and she moves closer to me, or should I say she *glides* closer to me, for Barbara Thorne has an elegance that far surpasses any woman I've ever met.

"I was across the way—out in the cemetery talking with Cyrinda when I... I don't know... I heard something? Felt something?"

"What exactly did you hear?"

"Kids laughing, I think. I don't know. I can't be sure. They were trying to talk to me."

Her eyes immediately light up and go wide with curiosity, and something else. Hope? Desire? Longing? "They?" she asks almost frantically.

I lower my head, lower my voice. "You think I'm crazy, don't you."

"Absolutely not!" she exclaims.

"I think it was the twins, Barbara. Your twins. David and Gretchen."

"In the cemetery? They spoke to you?"

"I… I don't know if it was *to* me, but they spoke. I heard muffled words. Crackly sounds. Like they were struggling to get through?" I sigh heavily. "I'm sorry!" I apologize. "I mean no disrespect, Barbara. It's rude to talk about them like this when I don't even know them or the situation or…"

She clutches the top of my shoulder and gives me a little excited shake. "It's not! It's fine! I'm just shocked that you were able to hear them! Ronnie! Ronnie! Come here!" she calls to the kitchen.

Ronnie comes bounding into the foyer with a red coffee mug in her hand. Her face screws up with curiosity when she sees us standing together. "What's going on?" she asks flatly, her high-pitched voice at one steady monotonic level. I can tell she's irritated at being summoned to see me.

"Trixie heard the twins. They spoke to her," Barbara announces.

"Well, not exactly, but…" I start to say.

There's an involuntary croaking noise from Ronnie's throat, and I can tell by the shift in her posture that she is further annoyed. "You did?" she asks surprised.

"I think?" I answer, unsure of myself.

"What did they say?" Barbara asks impatiently.

"I heard them say 'Blodheksa' a few times, something about the 'spawn of Satan.' They laughed. A lot."

Barbara's face lights up like she knows something, like she's remembering something, but Ronnie remains cold and stoic.

"'Innocent blood?'" I continue. "And something about the house of Arrah."

Barbara freezes. Whatever color is in her alabaster skin drains entirely like *she's* the one who's seen a ghost!

My hands are slick with nervous sweat, and I rub them down the sides of my jeans. "Is that bad?" I ask.

Ronnie eyes Barbara with an uncomfortable stare.

"No, no, Trixie," Barbara assures as her normal shade of pale returns to her face. "Arrah left a few days ago, but she's still *here*, if you know what I mean."

"She doesn't," Ronnie barks, and there's such a biting tone in her voice that it cuts into my ears with a painful gash.

"Rhonda!" Barbara scolds.

"She's right, though," I say defenselessly. "I don't."

Barbara places her other hand on my other shoulder. "It's okay. Nothing for you to worry about. The house of Arrah is where the children go on the astral plane. It isn't an actual place, per se, but it's the term they use to describe when they're unable to break through to me. They say they are at the house of Arrah."

"She's like their guardian?"

"More like a, like a safety net. She's a protector of all things on the astral plane."

"And she's working with you."

"Yes. She's been researching alongside me for a while now. She realized there's an astral code that needs to be solved before we can make the children flesh again. But until then, we need to keep… *experimenting*, so to speak."

"Like trying to bake a cake, but not having one of the ingredients," Ronnie says.

"Or taking it out of the oven too soon. Or leaving it in too long. We have the right recipe, but something is missing, and that's the part we're trying to figure out."

"Donna?" I ask.

"And June," Ronnie blurts, confirming my suspicions.

Barbara glares hard at her, and her shoulders shrink forward. "The fact that you heard the twins speaks volumes. It means we must be close. Their words have power and must be taken seriously. I told you your light was bright. They can sense you. You drew them out."

"Have you ever heard them, Ronnie?" I ask.

She glares at me the same way Barbara stared her down. Viciously. Angrily. I know the answer before I even ask the question, but a part of me wants to hear her admit it. Admit that *I* am more special than *she* is.

Barbara squeezes my shoulders and kisses my forehead. "Get to bed, Trixie. Think hard about what they said. I know you don't think they were speaking to you, but I promise you they were. Ronnie," she calls over, "defer to Trixie. If the children were trying to give her a message as to what to do next, we can't ignore it. Trust her. As a matter of fact, do what she says. I feel like we are so close to making this happen; we can't stop now. Full speed ahead, girls."

"Full speed ahead," Ronnie says unenthusiastically. She doesn't look me in the eye. If I'm assessing the situation correctly, it feels like she's just been dethroned.

I lead the pack now.

I call the shots.

And I will not let Barbara down in her mission. 'Cause this is my mission now, too. Barbara has spoken. The children have spoken. I will be the light and the truth and the way of the Crimson Coven now.

Chapter Fourteen

Sunday, June 6th 1965
June Taylor's House
517 West Elm Street
Salem, Illinois
Afternoon of the Half Moon

Kent called me the other day and asked if I would come to a vigil for June. I haven't spoken to or seen him since I quit working at the movie theatre! He called to tell me that June's mother was organizing a get-together for the community at the family home because all efforts to find June had come up fruitless (like I knew they would), and interest in the case was starting to wane. "Just another runaway" was the message the fuzz was riding on, but June's mom was insistent there was something more sinister at play and wanted to keep her daughter fresh in the memories of the people. I was hesitant at first, but eventually, I told him I would go. I was a little upset that it wasn't Clark who called me (I guess that ship has sailed). I was also surprised to learn that June's last name was Taylor, and that her mom's name, ironically, is Patricia. But then again, how would I have known that? June and I were barely a blip of friends, yet I'm posting flyers and attending candlelight vigils in her name? Makes me wonder even more about who's doing that for me. Makes me wonder who's taking up the mantle and leading the charge in search of Patricia Bluebell McGovern and her forever sidekick, Cyrinda. It took a little strong-arming to get Cyrinda to agree to come with me because she asserted that June was my friend and not hers and she would feel out of place. But when I told her we would feel out of place together, she relented and said she would join me.

Of course, I knew better. I knew the truth. I knew that all the efforts of Patricia Taylor to relocate and bring home her sweet daughter June were in vain. And because of that, Ronnie was pissy-faced when I asked her to give us a ride.

"You know there's a lot we need to do, Trix," she huffed at me. "Barbara said tonight would be a good night to…"

"I know," I said, "but this is something I need to do. I need to be there. It's something I really need to be a part of. Besides, don't you think it'll look weird if I *don't* show?"

Ronnie placed a hand on her hip and rocked back and forth, agitated. Her square jaw flexed at the cheekbones, and I knew she was holding something in. I knew she wanted to go off and explode on me, but Barbara had given her instructions to kinda do what I say, so…

She pointed her rigid forefinger at me. "If you say anything…" she began, her high-pitched voice lowering to a threatening octave.

"I'm not stupid, Ronnie," I said with an eyeroll. "Gosh. Do you think I would seriously betray Barbara like that?"

She sighed and bit her tongue. "Just don't slip up."

"Pinky promise," I said and to reassure her I held out my pinky finger for her to wrap around her own. Which she didn't.

She gave me a cold stare, turned on her heel, and muttered, "I'll be waiting in the car."

June's house is a sprawling white, two-story old farmhouse with a large wrap-around porch. As we pull up to it, I scan the faces of the people milling about and recognize none of them. Cyrinda clutches my shoulder from the back seat and whispers, "See. I told you it would be weird."

"Shhhh," I say forcefully.

"What did you say?" Ronnie asks.

"Nothing." I say dismissively.

"Listen, when you're ready to be picked up, walk over to the library on Maple and call me from there. Don't call me from the house."

"Wait. Why?"

"Just do it, Trixie. Trust me and do what I say."

"Fine, fine," I whine, and Cyrinda and I get out of the car.

"And remember…"

I put my hand up to my closed lips and make a turning gesture as if I'm locking up a treasure chest. Ronnie nods and pulls away.

"She has a serious problem," Cyrinda says.

"Yeah, well, she's just sour because Barbara favors me a little more now."

She sighs. "Oh, Trixie. When is this story going to end?"

My face twists at her odd choice of words. "I haven't the foggiest as to what you mean."

And there she is again … frightened little Cyrinda. She always rears her anxious little head at the most inopportune times. Her eyes are frantic with doubt, and the way the corners of her mouth practically slide off the sides of her face makes me seethe with anger. *Why can't she just be normal?* I scream on the inside. But I take a deep breath and pause for a second. "It's okay," I say sweeping her blonde hair behind her shoulder. "You were so brave when you had your little epiphany in the graveyard, remember? Let's stay the course. Let's stick to the plan. Me and you."

She smiles brightly. "You and me."

Me and my shadow.

And we head toward the front porch.

The second we begin to ascend the staircase, the screen door flies open violently, and Clark is there to greet us. My heart nearly jumps out of my chest, and those butterflies start dancing wildly in the pit of my stomach. I remember his kiss that day in Centralia—the way his rough tongue darted in and out of my mouth, the way his forceful hands groped at my chest, the way I was so close to lying down in the backseat and letting him have his way with me. Moisture surges between my legs and my cheeks get hot with embarrassment.

"Trixie!" he exclaims. "I didn't think you were going to come!"

I can't read him. I can't tell if he's genuinely surprised and happy I'm here, or if he's genuinely surprised but annoyed. I need to play this off and keep my cool. I can't look too eager or desperate or…

"Well, Kent called me, and I felt like I needed to be here. For support, of course," I say quickly.

Something in his eyes flickers. A spark. A glint. A glimmer. Like blue ice shimmering against the midday sun. He smiles and opens the screen door wider so we can enter the house. "Of course," he says. "Come. Mrs. Taylor wants to say a few words to the group. She made her famous cheesecake, too, so that'll be a treat."

I blush again, partially in embarrassment because I know nothing of Mrs. Taylor's cheesecake. "Thank you," I say and walk past him into the house. Cyrinda follows quickly behind me and doesn't say a word.

Everyone gathers in the living room. It's a large space with hardwood floors and fancy décor. I get the sense that this is a formal area of the home—not where the family hangs out and watches TV or anything like that. In fact, there's no TV here to be seen. Nope, this is one of those fancy rooms for ladies' tea and meetings of the Women's Auxiliary Club or some hoity-toity sorority. A stark contrast from the hippie-dippy Sisterhood stuff in Barbara's back den. Oh no, the Taylors are classy and have money, and judging by the amount of people in the room, they are well-connected. I look down at my dungarees and t-shirt and suddenly feel out of place. Like I'm drowning in a sea of vest dresses and pant-suits. I know Cyrinda feels the same way as she stays within a few inches of me.

Clark finds a spot on a couch and pats the space next to him for me to join. The furniture is much too nice for Cyrinda to perch herself on the arm, so she takes a spot on the floor in front of me and crosses her legs Indian style. I stroke the back of her hair, and she tilts her head up to smile at me. I am horrified by her visage. Her upside-down face is startling to look at—wide blue eyes beneath the umbrella of her tight smile. It throws me off, makes me feel uncomfortable, so I recoil my hands and place them in my lap.

Clark senses my uneasiness and reaches for my hand. "It's okay," he says. "We're the kids in this whole thing. Nobody cares about how you look. We're expected to dress like the teen-agers we are."

"Oh," I say, nervously. "Okay."

Mrs. Taylor swishes her way into the room in a grandiose manner with a stack of papers clutched tightly to her chest, and everyone stops talking. A quiet hush comes over the group as everyone abruptly ends their individual conversations so as to give her their full attention. I dart my head around the room to observe everyone who's here. So many faceless, nameless people. Mostly adults. Actually, I think Clark, Cyrinda, and I are the only teens here! "Where's Kent?" I whisper to Clark from the side of my mouth.

"Work. Julius needed him," he whispers back.

"What did he say?" Cyrinda chimes, but I give her back a little kick to shut her up.

"Thank you. Thank you all for coming out this afternoon," Mrs. Taylor addresses the crowd. "Friends and family, friends of June," she looks over at Clark with a strange, pained expression. "It hurts my heart for us to have to gather this way, for this reason, but as you all know, there has been no progress in locating my sweet June. The pain of not knowing where she is and the lack of new leads in her case have been unbearable. But today, I stand before you not just as a mother in pain but also as a member of this community that has the power to make a difference."

"Oh, she has the power alright," Clark mumbles, and an icy dread takes over my body. If Mrs. Taylor is as influential as Clark lets on, she's bound to dig up something or figure something out. And that *something* might lead her right back to Ronnie, and Barbara, and ultimately me. My hands go cold and clammy. Feverishly, I wipe them over my jeans, and Clark eyes me suspiciously. They all eye me suspiciously. Eyes close in on me, and I have the urge to run, run, run away. But I take a deep breath in and tell myself to be cool. Be cool. Be calm. Don't start to panic.

Mrs. Taylor passes out a new set of flyers to the group. "Our community has been supportive, and for that, I am truly grateful. However, I cannot ignore the fact that interest in June's story is starting to fade. It's crucial for us to keep the momentum going, to keep the search alive, and to bring June back home. I refuse to let my daughter become just another statistic, another forgotten face. Today, I want to present an action plan—a roadmap that each and every one of us can follow to reinvigorate the search for June."

"Get on with it, Deep Pockets," Clark mumbles again from the side of his mouth.

"Deep Pockets?" I ask. "What do you mean?"

"She's going to raise the reward amount, I bet." He says something else, but the words get muffled in my ears because he reaches over and squeezes the top of my knee. My body goes into a full-on spasm of lusty desire, and I can hardly concentrate on what Mrs. Taylor is saying. The room seems to stop, and I feel like I'm spinning. The mere touch of his hand in the most innocent of ways sends me over the moon. I think he notices. I think he notices my initial flinch and flutter because he smiles, and my body instinctively relaxes, accepting his touch.

"…headquarters in Cape Girardeau, Missouri, along the Mississippi River." Mrs. Taylor's voice bounds back into audible focus. *I know that city.* Clark had mentioned it when we went to Centralia.

For some reason, it resonates with me—makes me tune in back to what she's saying. Something about it feels … important and familiar at the very same time. My mind swirls with my own memories of childhood. Of me and Cyrinda playing in the backyard of the Marshall's home in Indiana. We were both fosters there for a while until we got placed in another home, and then another, and then another. But the Marshalls… that was an idyllic place. I wish we could have stayed there forever. "June loved going there in the summers, and it seems like a natural place to expand the search. By the end of the week, we'll be there, and the hotline number will be set up." Hearing Mrs. Taylor speak of Cape Girardeau stirred those feelings and thoughts inside me.

Clark's eyes shimmer again like they're reflecting back an unnatural light. He elbows me lightly. "Hey," he whispers. "Come with me."

Startled, I reply, "What? What do you mean? Mrs. Taylor is still…"

"It's fine. She doesn't care. It's the big wigs she's really talking to anyways."

I look around the room again at all the adult faces staring concernedly at Mrs. Taylor, hanging on to every word that comes out of her red-lipped mouth. "Why? Where are we going?"

"Just come on, it's a surprise!" He stands up and reaches for my hand.

I move to get up, and Cyrinda whips her head around with a scared, crazed expression.

"What's going on? Where are you going?" she asks frantically.

I lean forward and whisper, "Stay here. I'll be right back."

"What? Trixie, no! Don't leave me here!" Her voice shakes with pure terror.

"Just hang loose," I say. "I'll be a sec. Don't get all weird and conspicuous."

I turn my attention to Clark because I can't stand to see the desperation on her face. As I walk out the room, I hear a pathetic little squeaking sound come from her throat, and my heart drops for leaving her alone like that. But I have to admit, the guilty feeling lasts only so long, as I am extremely curious where Clark is taking me. We quietly leave the living room, and holding my hand, he guides me up the stairs to the second floor.

"What the hell?" I exclaim.

"Shhhhh…" he hushes me.

"Sorry, sorry," I say, lowering my voice.

"Here," he says as we come to a closed wooden door at the end of the long hallway. He pushes it open slowly so the creaking sound is lessened and guides me inside. "This is June's room."

The pink floral wallpaper matches the comforter set on the queen-sized bed, and everything is perfect and in place, and frilly with pink and white lace. At one point in time, I would have given anything to have a bedroom like this. I think I gasped because Clark lets go of my hand and says, "Yeah. Right? It sure is something."

Her room is stately. Like a princess's bedroom in a castle. I run my hand over the surface of the bedspread and breathe in the flowery scent that wafts in the air. "I take it you've been in here before?" I tease, remembering June telling me she had had a crush on Clark a while ago.

"Yeah, well, we've been friends for like, forever! Her parents always let all the kids hang out up in here."

"So, why are we here now?"

Clark ignores me and opens the bottom drawer of June's white wooden dresser and begins rummaging through it.

"Hey! What are you doing?" I say, agitated. It doesn't feel right watching him search through June's personal items.

He ignores me, shuts that drawer, goes to the next one, and does the same. An overwhelming need to protect June's privacy takes over me, and I get upset at his violation of her things. Pictures of little June at Cape Girardeau line the top of the dresser and practically scream at me to make him stop. "Clark!" I yell. "You really shouldn't be…"

"Hush, Trixie! I know she's got it in here somewhere."

I quickly move over to the dresser to try to see what he's searching for. I want to throw my arm out in front of him to stop his pursuit, but I am once again curious. "Got what?"

Suddenly, he pulls out a plastic baggie filled with a green, leafy substance. "This!" he boasts and dangles it in the space between us.

I exhale loudly, and my shoulders slump forward. Grass. He was looking for her drugs.

"I don't want her to get in trouble or anything. This was the only time I could sneak up here since she went missing." He sighs pensively. "I mean, I'm not giving up hope that she's coming home."

You should.

"Oh, of course not!" I chime.

"But if that is the case, I'm sure her mom will have to go through everything up here eventually. I wouldn't want her to find it."

I make my way to the bed and sit down on the edge. "Suuuuuurrrree," I say dragging out the word. "I know. You didn't want perfectly good reefer going to waste."

He gives me a sly smile and sits next to me. "Maybe."

I can't help but giggle as a silence falls between us. I keep my uncomfortable focus on my feet and watch as my legs dangle back and forth.

"Sooooo," he says, breaking the silence.

"So," I return.

"I just want to apologize for…"

"Stop," I cut him off. "You don't have to apologize."

"No Trixie. I'm sorry if things got too out of control that day. I'm sorry if it was too fast for you and all."

"It's fine," I say, trying to mask the knot in my throat. "What happened, happened. You never called me after the fact, so I pretty much know the score. Like I said, it's fine."

He shifts his body to face me and stares deeply into my eyes. "It's not fine. I'm sorry," he says, almost pleading with me. "That day. In the park. I don't know. I can't explain it. There was just something … weird? Magical?" He laughs nervously. "I don't know. Something about you was like a magnet. Like I couldn't control myself and… and I wanted to call, but I just couldn't bring myself to…"

"You don't have to make excuses or try to make me feel better," I interrupt.

"I'm not!" His eyes flash, and I notice that peculiar light shining back in them again. It looks like reflectors on a bicycle. I lean in closer to him to try to discern what it is exactly when he pulls the back of my neck towards him and kisses me deeply on the mouth.

I swoon. I reel. My whole body turns to jelly. Tingly, wiggly, jelly from my cheekbones all the way to my toes. I'm melting, I'm melting, like the Wicked Witch of the West. I'm on a rollercoaster ride and every loopty-loop of his tongue against mine sends waves of weightlessness in my soul, my stomach flipping and flopping like it would on each dip and drop of the ride. Soon his hand creeps up the bottom of my shirt, and my body tenses. He stops for a second and breaks our kiss. "I'm sorry," he says and quickly removes his hand.

"Don't be sorry." I try to reassure him because I don't want him to stop. I want to tumble into his arms on June's bed. I want to feel the weight of his body crashing down onto and into me. I want to feel his skin against my own.

He moves back in closer and kisses my neck. He runs his tongue up the side of it and takes my earlobe between his teeth. "What is it about you, Trixie?" he whispers heavily, sending chills down my back. "It's like there's a light in you that I'm drawn to. It pulls me in. Makes me want you so badly." He takes my hand and places it in his lap between his legs. His johnson rages against his jeans, practically begging me to release it. I rub my hands back and forth over the fabric of it, and he gives a little moan of pleasure in his throat.

My eyes flutter in ecstasy at his words, but then it hits me—*my light*. And Barbara's voice sings in my head. And Arrah's voice echoes through the space between Clark and me. And the twins start to giggle in the distance.

If you're not pure, they won't see your light.

Suddenly, I pull away from him and break from his embrace.

"What?" he asks breathlessly.

"I… I can't," I stammer.

He huffs and gets up from the bed—defeated, annoyed, and obviously unsatisfied *again*!

I jump up right behind him. "Come on, Clark! It's June's room! *June!* It's not right to carry on like this here."

'Cause it would be disrespectful to the dead…

"No, no," he relents. "You're right. This was a bad idea."

I swallow hard and suck in my pride. What does he mean *bad idea*? Bad idea to be here in June's room, or bad idea to be with *me*? I try so hard to hide my emotions from my face, but I don't think I do a very good job. "I'm gonna go," I mutter and walk out the door before he can respond.

I quickly trot down the stairs and peek my head into the living room threshold. Cyrinda sees me in the doorway, and I mouth to her, "Let's go."

She gets up from the floor and follows me out the front door. "What happened? What was that all about?" she asks when we step off the front porch.

"Nothing," I say. "Clark needed to get his pot from June's room."

"Did you smoke any?"

"Oh, hell no!" I exclaim.

"So, what happened up there? What took you so long?"

"Nothing. Nothing," I say, brushing it off. "Come on. We gotta go to the library down the street so we can call Ronnie to get us. We gotta go home."

Chapter Fifteen

Sunday, June 6th 1965
Barbara's Chevy Impala
Salem, Illinois
Afternoon of the Half Moon

The red Impala screeches to a dead stop at the corner of Maple. We waste no time and practically sprint over to it. "Get in the back. Now!" Ronnie commands.

I open the back door for Cyrinda to get in first, but I inspect the curious passenger in the front seat before I hop in. A young woman wearing a paisley sundress is slumped up against the door. Her brown hair poofs out at the sides from underneath an oversized beige, floppy hat. I can't tell if she's sleeping or…

"Quit yer staring and get the hell in already!" Ronnie barks.

Dumbstruck, I obey and sit pretty close to Cyrinda.

"Is… is… is she…" I begin.

"No," Ronnie snaps back. "Not yet, at least." She peels out as soon as the door clicks shut and vrooms down the street like a bat out of hell. The woman in the front moans slightly, giving me confirmation that she is in fact *not* deceased.

"Who is she?" Cyrinda asks meekly. She's clearly unnerved by Ronnie. Always has been. Cyrinda never quite had the same interactions with her as I did, and there was always a weird tension thing between the two of them. It was as if Ronnie ignored Cyrinda whenever she was around. I know Ronnie has a kinda beef with me, more so predicated on jealousy, but with Cyrinda? It was a complete non-acknowledgment.

"Ronnie?" I say, raising my voice over the roar of the engine. "Ronnie, who's the skirt?"

She squints at me in the rearview mirror. "Well, you would know if you were with me to help," she sneers.

"What do you mean?"

The young woman moans again like she's regaining consciousness and Ronnie steps on the gas propelling the car into a violent lurch.

"You drugged her?" I yell in disbelief.

Ronnie sighs loudly. "Well, yeah! What was I supposed to do? I was alone because you weren't there to help me!" She takes the next right turn too wide and jumps the curb.

Cyrinda tugs on the bottom of my shirt. "Trix! Ronnie drugged that girl? Why?"

"I really coulda used your help, Trixie," Ronnie continues her tirade, not allowing me to answer Cyrinda. "But you just had to go to that stupid vigil when you know damn well where that June girl is!"

Cyrinda punches my upper arm lightly. "Trixie!" she wails excitedly. "What is she talking about?"

"Shush up for a second, will ya?" I scold.

"What did you say?" Ronnie yells, and the woman in the front stirs again. "Fuck! She's almost out of it."

I inch my butt to the edge of the seat and wiggle my way through the opening to the front. I lean forward and point out the window. "We're almost there," I reassure.

"I know, Patricia!" she says condescendingly. "You don't think I know where we are?"

"I'm sorry, *Rhonda*," I retort. "I had to go. It would have looked suspicious if I didn't. They asked me to be there. I had no other choice."

Ronnie gives one last hard turn on the steering wheel, and I swear I feel she's going to flip the car over. Cyrinda digs her nails into my side as she holds on to my waist.

"You always have a choice, Trixie. Always," Ronnie mumbles, but I get the sense that she's talking to herself more than she's talking to me. She throws the car in park when we get to the front of Barbara's house. "Help me get her out!"

I make a move to exit, but Cyrinda tugs harder on me, holding me back. She looks at me, bewildered and confused. "What is happening right now?" she asks.

I suck in my breath and pause, trying to fish in my brain for the right words. *I know what's about to happen. I know where we're taking the girl and why.* But I need to shelter Cyrinda from this awful truth for just a little longer. Just until I've helped Barbara bring the children back. Just until I've secured our spot in the new world. Then I can tell Cyrinda the whole truth and nothing but the truth.

"I'm not one hundred percent sure," I lie. "But I think this has something to do with that thing Barbara asked me to help her with."

Cyrinda stiffens and opens her mouth to say something, but Ronnie yells at me again. "Come on, man! Let's boogie!"

"Just go to our room. I'll be there in a bit," I say to Cyrinda as I get out of the car.

I don't even look back to catch her expression. I proceed to stand to the side of Ronnie as she scoops the woman up under one of her shoulders. Dipping my own shoulder low, I catch the woman in her armpit and help Ronnie whisk her away to the basement.

"It's broad daylight, ya know!" I scold.

"Yeah, well, it would have been much easier with your help," she growls back.

"I told you why I couldn't be there. You could have waited until I was done."

"I had an open opportunity that I couldn't miss. It was then or never. It's the half-moon, ya know? This was a golden moment!"

"I know it's the half-moon! I'm not an idiot, Ronnie!"

"Well, you're totally acting like…"

"Girls! Girls!" Barbara yells from the basement. "What's all the bickering about?"

Ronnie and I close our mouths like two fighting sisters being chastised by their mother and eye each other with disdain. Barbara is wrapped in her white robe, ready for the afternoon ritual. Her hair is swirled tightly in a bun, and poking out from the sleeves of the robe I can see her flesh is decorated with the drawings of the runes again. I wonder what they say. What ancient spells does she write on her body? Does Barbara know what they mean? I mean, she has to, right? She's been a witch for many years. No. Not a witch. A *heksa*. She taught me that word.

"Nothing Barbara, nothing," Ronnie says.

Barbara nods at her and turns to me. "Trixie?" she says, probingly.

"Like Ronnie said. It's nothing."

She gives us a suspicious look. Her eyes flash to bright blue for a moment, then quickly return to chocolate brown. She points to the empty chair in the middle of the room, in the middle of the pentagram drawn in chalk on the cement floor, and Ronnie and I drag the woman over, set her down in it, and bind her with thick knotted rope.

Her head sways to the left and her floppy hat falls to the floor revealing her mass of brown, bouncy curls. It reminds me of an ocean of chocolate tumbling in perfumed waves. She smells clean. Sterile. Like she meticulously takes care of herself—hair, nails, makeup, perfume, fashionable clothing. Not at all like your typical runaway tramp or wannabe movie star who cleans herself in truck stop bathrooms, wears garish makeup to hide her sad smile, and douses herself in cheap perfume to mask her unbathed scent. No, this one was different. This one wasn't feral like the others. Ronnie scarcely notices Barbara raising her eyebrows when the woman's eyes start to flutter open, but I do. I distinctly take note of Barbara's growing contempt as the prisoner comes to.

Barbara crinkles her nose as she circles the chair. Ronnie nervously shifts back and forth on her heels. "Something wrong, Barbara?" she asks.

"Hmmm," Barbara sings pensively. "I can't rightly say yet. Something is…" She pauses, breathes in the air around the woman, sucks in hard with her nose like a bloodhound sniffing out its prey and exhaling slowly from her mouth. "Off."

Ronnie wrings her hands together. Her anxiety is palpable, and something inside me gets delightfully giddy.

"W… where… am… I?" the woman quietly asks as she adjusts her vision to her damp, cement surroundings.

Barbara's head snaps to Ronnie, and Ronnie walks to the woman and double checks the security of the rope.

The woman's eyes shoot open when she understands she is trapped in place. Frantic.

Furious. But mostly scared and confused. "What are you doing, Allie?" she mumbles to Ronnie. "Where did you bring me?" Tears begin to stream down her cheeks—silent tears of realizing she's made a very, very big mistake.

"It's fine," Ronnie says trying to relax her. "It'll all be over soon."

The woman jolts in the chair, lifting it a few centimeters from the ground. "What do you mean 'over soon?'" she screams desperately. She swivels her head to look at Barbara then at me. "Please! Please help me! I have to go home. I need to go home."

Barbara raises her hand, and something in the woman's eyes goes dark. Vacant. Quiet. Her body relaxes against the restraints like she's been drugged again—silenced. Slack-jawed, her head wobbles forward, and it's clear to see she has no control over her limbs.

"I don't know what I..." Ronnie begins, but Barbara silences her too with a sharp "shush."

"But Trixie wasn't there with me to help, and so this was the best that I could..." she continues, speaking faster and more nervously.

"I said to be quiet, Rhonda!" Barbara yells, and the whole house seems to shake at its very base.

Ronnie's mouth tightens, and she takes a step backward out of the glow of the overhead chain light.

Again, Barbara walks around the woman, smelling the delicate air within the pentagram. She circles round and round her so many times that I almost find myself in the same trance. The temperature shifts in the room. It's thick and heavy, like right before a rainstorm on a summer day. Barbara pulls a lock of the woman's hair and holds it up to the lamplight, inspecting the dark strand. She hems and haws for a moment, then wraps the hair tightly around her pinky finger. "You don't want to stay here with me?" she softly sings to the woman.

The woman shakes her head.

Barbara feigns a pout. "Oh? Why not? That hurts my feelings."

More tears silently slide down the woman's face. "I'm sorry. I'd love to stay. It's so pretty here. But I need to get home. Someone's waiting for me." Her voice is like the voice in a dream. Faraway. Empty and longing.

"Oh?" Barbara repeats calmly. "Who's waiting for you?"

The woman's face brightens at her thoughts like a lightbulb's rays breaking through the darkness of Barbara's spell. She smiles. "Belinda," she says fondly.

"And who is Belinda?" Barbara asks.

"Belinda," the woman repeats. "My girl. My little baby girl."

"She has a child?" I whisper, but it was really supposed to be an inside thought.

Immediately, Barbara snaps the hair off from her finger and drops it onto one of the candle's open flames. It sizzles and sputters and leaves a foul, acrid scent behind. She marches over to

Ronnie, grabs her by the elbow, and drags her up the basement steps.

Through the floorboards, I can vaguely make out what Barbara says, but it's apparent she's quite angry with Ronnie. I hear her say things like, "It's not even her moontime!" and "You screwed this one up!" and "You should have known she had a child!"

Ronnie scrambles to justify her actions, and the bits that do come through seem like she's trying to throw me under the bus. Like it's all my fault because I wasn't with her when she snatched the woman, but I can tell Barbara isn't jiving with it. Barbara says something about "pureblood" and "opening the veil," but that still doesn't make much sense to me.

They move their argument back to the top of the steps, and I can hear more clearly. Ronnie promises to clean up the mess but says that things are getting too risky. "We're going to have to leave soon, Barbara." To which Barbara doesn't respond. I hear her footfalls across the kitchen floor and into the back of the house where her bedroom is.

Ronnie doesn't come back down right away, so curiously, I move closer to the woman. The woman tied up in the chair. The brown-haired, doe-eyed woman with her sweet Belinda waiting for her at home. All she wants is to get back to her little girl—leave this place behind, forget any of this ever happened, and continue on with her normal life.

You don't know how close you came, I say to her in my head.

She looks up at me with a pained expression. "Will you help me? Please?" she whispers her plea to me.

"It's okay. Someone will take you home," I say, trying to reassure her so she doesn't go off into a fit of panic.

"Thank you," she mouths and tilts her head back like she's once again in some timeless trance.

"Where is home, honey?" I ask, but the thought pops into my head that she probably will not make it back to wherever home is. "Tell me, so I can get you there."

"The Cape," she whispers again. "Cape Girardeau."

Suddenly my world stops.

Flashes of June's bedroom pictures come bounding into my vision. Her mother's voice echoes in my head. Cape Girardeau. The place June held so dear. The place her family visited year after year on carefree family trips. The place her family will soon set up as their headquarters to continue their search for her. It's the city of endless summer and hot dogs and ice cream and children... so, so many children. The land of permanent vacation! And as if everything seems to fall into place, I know. I know what I have to do. I know how I'll be able to help Barbara. It comes so clearly to me. There is something that's calling me there. To that place. To that spot.

Cape Girardeau.

I hear the name of the city echo in my head. Or maybe the woman just said it a second time. I can't be sure. But the sound of it strengthens my resolve, and a plan begins to unfurl in my mind. I see it floating in mid-air. A map with frayed edges and a dashed line connecting Salem, Illinois to Cape Girardeau, Missouri. And just to the left of the Mississippi River is a red X. It pulsates on the warped map paper—glowing and beckoning me to go there. There. To the red X. Like the one on Trent's forehead in the car. I don't know why I remember that at that very moment, but I do. Trent. Galen. Whoever he was and is. He brought me here to Barbara and Ronnie, and for some reason, I feel like he's bringing me to Cape Girardeau.

I blink my eyes rapidly to get myself out of my head. "What's your name?" I ask her.

"Trina," she mumbles. She's still in that weird in-and-out state—still feeling the effects of Barbara's spell.

"Okay, Trina from Cape Girardeau. I'm going to make sure you'll get home safe and sound and back to Belinda. All of this will soon be a distant nightmare. How old is Belinda?" I ask, trying to keep her mind on something positive.

"Two. She's two." Trina half smiles at me, and I smile back as my plan opens wider and wider in my consciousness.

Barbara didn't want Trina because she's a mother. She has a child who relies on her. A young child. She doesn't want to separate mothers from their children.

But what if she's got it all wrong?

What if it's not the women she needs to complete the spell?

What if it's the children themselves?

And Trina is going to bring us right to her precious little one...

"Trixie!" Ronnie yells from the top of the stairs. "What the hell are you doing?"

"Nothing!" I yell over my shoulder, but my eyes remain fixated on Trina.

Ronnie trots down the steps. Her footfalls are like thunder against the rug-less wooden planks. "Why are you talking to her?"

"Because, Ronnie. We have to help her."

Ronnie jerks my shoulder and spins me around to meet her face. She draws in closer to me and talks out of the corner of her mouth. Under the lamplight, her short black hair looks like an oil slick on the side of the road. An oil slick in the night that reflects back all the green and purple colors of the sticky, wet substance. Ronnie has always intrigued me. Always...

"Ixnay on the elp-hay," she mumbles. "You know what we have to do."

"But what if we don't?" I counter.

"Excuse me?" she crows. "You know damn well we can't just drop her off at the bus station! Or better yet, let's just give her a lift back home!" She laughs with a condescending tone like I must be the biggest idiot in the world.

"Well, why not?"

She pulls away from me, and her eyes practically bulge out of their sockets. "Are you warped, Trixie? The second she gets her footing on solid ground, she's gonna give up everything, and we're done for. Done. For. Ya dig?"

"But what if she doesn't? What if this is an opportunity to actually make some progress?"

Ronnie's hands jerk to her hips and a sneer overtakes her face. "Oh yeah? Trixie got a big plan or something? Tell me, Trix. What you got cookin' in that head of yours?"

"I don't know. It just seems like all of this is connected."

"Connected how?"

"June, Trina, her kid, Barbara. All of it. We gotta take Trina back home to Cape Girardeau."

"What do you mean, *gotta*?" she scoffs.

"C'mon, Ronnie," I begin to plead. "Remember Barbara told you to follow my lead not too long ago?"

Her face darkens with the memory, and her head gives the slightest of nods like she doesn't want to fully acknowledge that I have rank over her.

"Well," I continue, "I just have a feeling. I can't explain it, but more than anything, I have this sense that we need to get to Missouri. It's all connected."

"Oh yeah? And what are we gonna do once we get out there?"

"I'm not entirely sure. But I know we have to get Trina back to her girl. I feel like the kid is the key to unlocking all of this."

I remember what the twins said to me in the graveyard! They were giving me a message!

"Unlock all what?"

"For Barbara. Like, I feel like whatever is in Missouri is going to be the thing to help Barbara get the twins back. To bring them back to life. Jesus Christ! That sounds so stupid when you say it out loud. Didn't you ever think that?"

"Think what?" she responds, her voice softening.

"How ridiculous this whole thing is. How just saying 'bring the twins back to life' is so ludicrous."

"I used to," she answers looking at the ground. "But then I saw the truth."

You are the truth and the light and the way, Barbara's voice echoes in my mind.

"I saw the things that Barbara can do," Ronnies continues. "And I pledged to be by her side to the very end. Much like you did, Trixie." She glares up at me hard as her jaw clenches at the sides of her chiseled face.

"Oh, I know. I'm with you. I'm with Barbara. That's a fact, Jack! All I'm saying is we should explore other options and other alternatives. And my gut is telling me that Trina is an option. Taking Trina home is a very viable, possible option."

"She's gonna tell, Trixie. That's what people do. They like their stories and gossip and boogeymen.

She'll rat us out. The first chance she gets. Mark my words."

"I don't think so. We have leverage. Her daughter. I feel like we need to get to Belinda first. Then you can take care of Trina however you need to, but getting the girl should be our first objective."

'Cause if my gut is telling me what I think my gut is telling me, Barbara needs a *child* sacrifice to complete the ritual. The twins need child blood to manifest again.

Chapter Sixteen

Saturday, June 12th 1965
The Downtowner Motel
Morgan Oak Street, Cape Girardeau, Missouri
Night of the Waxing Gibbous Moon

Up close and personal, the Mississippi River is huge. I mean, I learned all about it in school, but when I actually got to see it with my own two peepers, well, let me tell ya, it sure is something else. God only knows what secrets are at the bottom of that beast! Cape Girardeau is just on the west side of it, and when we crossed it, it seemed like it sang. To me. For me. I asked Cyrinda if she heard anything as we went over it, and she said no. I didn't dare ask Ronnie. She was so royally pissed off the entire ride that she barely said anything to anyone. Thankfully, she stuck Trina in the front so as to keep a "watchful eye" on her and make sure she remained unconscious the whole two hours. Cyrinda and I happily took the back seat. But I call bullshit on the arrangement. I think Ronnie was so angry with me—so burnt with jealousy—that she didn't want me to be next to her. Whatever camaraderie Ronnie and I had been trying to salvage had completely melted away when Barbara sided with me and when I decided on the Cape Girardeau plan. For all these months, Ronnie had been Barbara's right-hand man, and now… well, Barbara was exploring other options. And those other options lead straight to me.

Barbara had told me that I was the piece of the Crimson Coven that had been missing and that I was going to be the one to help her. I need to fulfill that debt, that obligation to her. She protected me—took me in, gave me shelter and food, listened to my problems, treated me like a real daughter, hell, she even saved my innocence and quite possibly my life from Carny John. I *had* to strive for her. I *had* to fight for her. I *had* to show her that I was worthy of her love and devotion.

Somehow, Ronnie had finagled a way to get one of the guys at her job to lend her his car. A 1965 Ford Thunderbird! It's a tough car and the engine roars when you accelerate. Ronnie calls it "thunder kissing," but I've never heard anyone use that term before. I think she was just joshing with me to make me feel stupid. Anyhow, the dagone car is brand new, and it makes me wonder what kind of spell Ronnie had to put on the guy to get him to give it to her. Maybe she did some sexual favors for him? 'Cause Ronnie isn't the friendliest of people, so I'm guessing something had to be given in return. Regardless, Barbara said we had to get our own vehicle, so we did. Ronnie did.

Barbara said a lot of things to Ronnie before we left, and that's part of the reason Ronnie is so ticked. In all my time at the house on Shelby, I had never seen Barbara as livid as she was the day the "Trina Incident" went down. Ronnie had pouted and cried and said things like, "I'm sorry I can't be like your pure and precious Patricia," which, of course, she knew I heard her say. I mean, I was right there in the basement for Pete's sake!

But all Barbara kept screaming over and over was "Fix it, Ronnie! Just fix it!" And when she hollered, the whole house stood still. Heck, I think the whole *world* stood still! When her voice rose, it felt like my ears clogged up with water, or like I was in some kind of sound-proof bubble in outer space because there was no other sound but the sound of her voice. And the sound wasn't just her voice, but it came up from the depths of her stomach and pulled the voices of other witches, (I mean heksas), from all ends of the earth to join together and come out of her mouth. Like, she commanded them to speak through her. She *willed* them to speak in her voice. Ronnie was scared. It was obvious from her movements throughout the house. Her fear was palpable even through the floorboards above me as she paced back and forth. But I can't deny that I, too, was afraid. Even though Barbara has always told me not to be afraid, that time, I legitimately was.

It was all very surreal.

Speaking of surreal, I also had to wonder about Trina and what was going to happen next with her. Between the spell Barbara put on her and the constant influx of chloroform, to the average person, it appeared that the girl in the front seat with the floppy hat and hippy dress was just merely sleeping. When we checked into The Downtowner Motel, and the clerk eyed us suspiciously, we told him that Trina was our sorority sister who had had too much to drink, and we needed to sober her up right quick. Then we dragged her up the flight of steps, into the room, and dumped her onto one of the double beds. Ronnie's been huffing and mumbling ever since we got here.

"What are we going to do with her?" I ask for about the hundredth time. But it's at this point I realize we never really bothered to come up with a good plan to use Trina to get to Belinda. We don't know where the kid is, who is with her, or if anyone is looking for Trina at this point.

Ronnie lights another cigarette and takes a long drag. The orange glow from the tip of it sizzles loudly as she deeply inhales. I feel like the sound echoes in the room, and for some reason, it makes me uneasy. The crackle of the cigarette paper is almost like Ronnie's brain crackling with her intent. I fear what she's going to say.

"Barbara told me to fix it, so that's what I'm gonna do." Another deep, long drag. I swear, I think she burned her lungs with that one!

"But fix it how?" I press, also realizing that Ronnie isn't even aware of the whole "child murder" thing.

"Look, Trixie, I know you think you got this whole thing figured out or something. And for whatever reason, Barbara has put her utmost faith in you. But you have to understand something," she pauses, turns the cigarette around to inspect the tall line of gray ash that has built up at the tip, and flicks the end of it with her thumb so that the ashes float down to the carpet. "I've been doing this a long time. I know how this all goes. I know how this all plays out. After I take care of Trina, I'm gonna go to the drug store and get you hair dye."

"Hair dye! Why?"

"I'm going to cut mine shorter and dye yours black, so we can't be identified. We have to cover all our tracks. Then I'll touch base with Barbara and see what's what."

"You didn't answer my question, Ronnie! What about Trina? What about her kid? We agreed to…"

"I didn't agree to nothing, Trixie! I don't know what you're thinking about or why you're so obsessed with this kid of hers."

"Barbara seemed to think it was important."

Her eyes go wide with shock and surprise. "She did?" she crows. "That's news to me! Are you sure we heard the same conversation?"

I lower my head and bite my tongue. I don't want to tell Ronnie why I know Trina's daughter is going to be advantageous to us 'cause she'll just yell at me some more.

"I'll probably just take her to the River. It's probably the fastest and easiest."

"I don't know, Ronnie," I say in a soft voice, because I *do* know.

"You see that full moon out there?" she asks, pointing to the large picture window in our motel room. More ash falls to the carpet as she waves the cigarette back and forth.

I move over to the window and pull the curtain slightly to the side just so the sky is in my line of vision. *She's mistaken*, I think. *It's still waxing. There's a super thin line of darkness that rims the corner and...*

"And that means it's the perfect time to get this done," she finishes.

I can't understand how someone so committed to and immersed in this lifestyle can be so blatantly wrong about something so important. Heck! I even know the moon is not in its full cycle yet, and Ronnie doesn't?

Trina stirs on the bed. She stutters and mutters what comes off as incomprehensible at first, but as I listen closely, I realize she's calling out for her daughter. For Belinda. Ronnie stamps the cigarette out in the orange ashtray and scurries over to her.

"Jesus Christ!" she exclaims and fishes in her pocket for her chloroform-soaked handkerchief to hold it over Trina's mouth until she's no longer squirmy. "I can't keep doing this, ya know!" she roars in agitation. "I gotta take care of this, Trixie. My way."

"Mmmhmm," I mumble, half-paying attention. A light from outside the window catches my attention, and curiosity draws my eyes away from the scene on the bed.

"That should do it for now," Ronnie says as she walks over to the door. "I'm gonna go see if I can get us a bite or something. If she wakes up again, just try to keep her as calm as possible, you dig?"

"Mmmhmm," I repeat.

"Trixie! I'm serious! Did you even hear a word I said?" she yells at me like I'm a child.

I shift my eyes sharply to meet hers so as to validate what she said. "Food. Back soon. Keep her calm if she wakes. Roger that." I'm short and to the point because I want her to just leave. Get out of here and leave me alone!

Ronnie puts one hand on her hip and sighs. It's such a Barbara-like gesture, and I think that Ronnie must have watched Barbara make that same gesticulation hundreds of times that she just naturally picked up on it and adopted it as her own. She huffs a deep sigh and shakes her head in disgust and disapproval. "I'll be back."

"Mmmhmm," I say again and turn away from the door.

The light from outside flashes again. It's not the moon or the stars or even the streetlights from the block over. Curious, I pull the curtain back again and stare out into the darkness. But the darkness isn't so dark. It isn't so desolate. It's Cape Girardeau—June's favorite vacation spot, according to her mother, Patricia. And it's filled with the sound of children.

The back of the hotel butts up directly against the residential houses on the next street. Our room just so happens to overlook the backyards of the people who live there. There aren't any fences to separate the property lines, so the individual yards look like one big giant piece of land that the children run aimlessly back and forth in as they play a game of hide-and-go-seek. The summer grass crunches under their bare feet—I can hear it distinctly through the panes of glass—and they howl and cheer with delight when someone is tagged, and someone is found, and someone reaches "home base" unscathed. Their laughter is infectious, and I smile in spite of myself.

"Whatcha looking at?" Cyrinda inquires.

Geez, I'd forgotten that she was even here. She always gets tight-lipped around Ronnie because I know Cyrinda doesn't care much for her. Can't say I blame her…

"Kids playing in the back," I answer and move over a little so Cyrinda can see.

"Oh," she sings, "that's nice. Remember those days? You and me. Dancing around like wild children playing all kinds of games. There's a whole gaggle of them out there. With us, it was just *us*, and that was always kinda nice, wasn't it?"

"Yeah," I answer contemplatively, but my remembrance is cut short by the flashing light again. "Hey! Did you see that?"

"See what?" Cyrinda asks confused.

"There was a light down there. It flashed so bright; how could you have missed it?"

She shrugs. "I dunno. I must have blinked. They might be playing with a flashlight."

I look out again, trying to locate the source. "No. I don't think they are. It's just one light. It came from the back porch of that house right there, shut off, came back to the porch and…" I pause when I see it race back and forth across the grass. "Look at that! Tell me you don't see it! It's magnificent! I can't describe it!"

Because I can't. The light is white and oh-so-bright. So bright I feel like I'll go blind if I look at it for too long. It radiates and pulses and flickers like a jar of lightning bugs flittering about. I'm mesmerized by it. Drawn to it. I feel like I fall into the light the longer I stare. I feel like the light will open up the sky like the light in Barbara's bedroom, or the light in the den during my initiation. I want to be in that light. I want to touch it, to drink it, to bathe in it, to wrap my arms around it and will it to life in the form of the twins. Gretchen and David. David and Gretchen. How happy would Barbara be if I went back home with the children reformed! Then we could be one big happy family and…

"Where are you right now?" Cyrinda says, interrupting my thoughts. "It's just a bunch of kids playing outside. There's no light, Trix. Just the one coming from the house they keep going in and out of."

At Cyrinda's words the light flickers like a light bulb struggling to stay on. Right before the power surges, and all the lights in the house blink with the death knell of lost power. As it does, I see the shape of a little girl. She can't be more than two or three years old. She flitters around in the grass, half playing with her siblings, half playing a game on her own. I blink a few times and take in her visage. Darling little girl with soft blonde hair and the biggest set of dimples indented on her cheeks.

"Bethy!" one of the others calls to her, and before she takes off running, she looks over in my direction. Right up at the window. She looks me directly in the eyes and smiles. And when she smiles, she lights up again—a ball of energy sparkling like the Fourth of July.

"Look at her!" I say out loud, but not meaning to. "She's so bright and pure! I need to get that light for Barbara." My voice trails off to a far-away place, and I no longer have any perception of day or time.

"Trixie!" Cyrinda scolds. "What the heck are you saying?"

"Barbara. I know she could use that light to bring her babies back. Mold it. Sculpt it. Barbara can do anything she wishes. She's made of fire, you know. Fire and October and wild leaves in the graveyard. She has the soul of the most powerful witch—the one who raised the dead back in the day."

"No, Trixie! Cut it out! You're talking cra..." Suddenly she stops herself in mid-sentence and sighs. Her shoulders slump forward in defeat and her face turns hard and serious. "I know, Trixie. I'm not stupid. Nor am I blind, or deaf, or dumb."

I turn my head to look at her, and I'm taken off guard by her change in demeanor, my face twists in knots that hurt the sides of my cheeks. "What do you mean?" I ask, squinty-eyed and pouty-lipped.

"You can stop pretending or hiding or whatever it is you think you're doing. Keeping me in the dark isn't protecting me, Trixie. Shutting me out doesn't shield me from anything."

"Cyri, I…" I start, but she cuts me off.

"I had an inkling early on. An inkling about what was happening at Barbara's. And I was just so happy to see you feel comfortable and wanted and loved. And you were so happy. So at ease. So open to a new way of life and of starting over. But it runs deeper than the surface stuff, Trix. It's evil and sinister. I was hoping you would eventually see that, and we would walk away from it all, but you continued to immerse yourself."

I put my hands on my hip and defiantly shift my weight from one side to the other. "Evil? Cyrinda, we've had this conversation before," I chastise.

"Kinda. Maybe. But we've never talked about it openly because I wasn't a hundred percent on what was what. But I know—the Crimson Coven, June, Donna, and the countless other girls—runaways like us who were sacrificed—*killed*—for some twisted ceremony. It's a horror movie, Trixie. I thought you would be able to see that eventually. But you're too deep, and I don't think I can pull you out of it this time."

"You think too much," I say coldly, flatly, and the light from outside shines directly into the room. I stare at it, hypnotized for a brief moment as I feel my consciousness careening into a dark void. I hear music in the distance. The music that played so often at Barbara's house. It comforts me, makes me feel safe and protected. When I look at Cyrinda, the light consumes the outline of her figure, and she blinks out of existence for a second. Like she flashed away. I blink my eyes to adjust to the darkness of the room and the over-powering light shining in, and she's there again, standing in front of me with a pained expression on her face.

"Oh, there you are. I thought you left," I say absentmindedly.

"What are you talking about? Do you even hear the words coming out of your mouth?" she pleads.

"Forget it, you wouldn't understand," I say dismissively and move back over to the window. My heart leaps at the thought of getting lost in the light, and all I can concentrate on is how I am going to obtain it for myself … and for Barbara.

"I know what you're thinking," she says.

"No, you don't," I say curtly.

"Yes, I do. I always know. You want to take that child. Whatever you see in her, you want to drain it from her. And there's only one way to do that…"

"Whatever I see in her? I don't understand how you can't see how bright she burns! Bethy!" I sigh her name like a lullaby.

"Maybe because I wasn't initiated in your coven? Maybe because you've kept me in the dark for so long. A shadow in the shadows."

"Oh, don't be so dramatic! Maybe if you put yourself out there and actually *communicated* with people…" I look over my shoulder as the light flickers in the room again. As Cyrinda flickers in and out of my vision again. My stomach turns to a block of ice, and I shake my head back and forth to relieve myself of the sickening feeling of doom and loneliness. "Jesus Christ! Would you stop doing that!" I scream.

Cyrinda's face screws up in confusion. "Doing what?" she asks innocently.

"Forget it, forget it," I say and look back out the window.

"Trixie? How did we get here? What is this? What's going on?"

"We're starting a new life, Cyrinda. The best way we know how. And we're a part of something so much larger than ourselves. It's like destiny. Like fate. All the stars and lights and planets aligned to bring us here. To the here and now."

"To the nowhere," she mumbles, but I pretend like I didn't catch that.

"What did you say?" I ask.

"Nothing, nothing." She pauses for a moment as I continue to drown myself in the pure and innocent light of little Miss Bethy behind my motel room. I dream of all the glorious ways to trap this firefly in a bottle and all the ways Barbara will be able to extract that energy from her. I can almost hear Gretchen and David laughing in their picture, laughing in their graveyard. The music fills my head, and I start to swoon.

"Trixie?" Cyrinda says after god knows how long.

"Mmmhmm," I respond.

"When this is all done and over with, I'm leaving. I'm going back to Indianapolis."

"Okay," I say, unaffected by her words.

"I'm serious, Trix. This isn't for me. And I know we promised and all, but…"

"Okay," I repeat, my insides numb and cold. Normally, I would have protested and yelled and screamed, and did everything in my power to convince Nervous Nelly Cyrinda that it is a shitty idea.

But the light is so bright, and I just don't care about what she says…

"You definitely don't need me anymore. I just figure I'll hitch a ride back or something."

"Just make sure it isn't someone like Trent," I say sarcastically. "Or Ronnie for that matter."

"Where are you, Trixie?" she asks, her voice drained and at the point of surrender.

"I'm in the light, Cyrinda. Where are you?"

"I guess I'm still in the shadows, Trix," she says, defeated.

"Exactly."

Chapter Seventeen

Sunday, June 13th 1965
The Downtowner Motel
Morgan Oak Street, Cape Girardeau, Missouri
Afternoon of the Waxing Gibbous Moon

There is no time as I am transfixed, dare I say, bewitched. I stared all night long out the motel window. Stared until my eyes filled to the brim with tears. I would blink a few times to release the liquid from the sides of them, and then continue to look and watch and wait. I knew not what I waited for, but I knew there was a silent anticipation in the air that propelled me to stare. Stare. Stare. I stared so hard that I think I physically left my body. My spirit floated outward and upward and downward into the backyard of the children who played. My soul tried to track the light of the little one, and I was happiest when I was able to be enveloped in it. I couldn't see her face or form or figure, but the light of her innocence burned. Burned. Burned. Hot and deep and true. But not a painful burn. It was a kind of burn that was satisfying, like scratching an itch. It left me wanting more every time I had to blink my eyes and clear the staring tears away. Her light was like pure energy pulling me closer and closer.

"Bethy," the other children had called her. *Bethy*. And I thought about what Trent and Barbara had said about *me*—that *my* light was bright too. My light of purity and innocence and wonder. *Is that what people saw when they looked at me?* I didn't know. I didn't care. All I could do was stare. Stare. Stare. And pretend to be in that aura of her light.

Ronnie had come back at some point. She had barked some directives at me, cursed at me a little bit, then huffed out of the room hauling Trina under her arm. When Ronnie came back later on, she put a bag of food, some pop bottles, and a bag with drug store hair dye on the little motel table and left again. Trina wasn't with her. I think. I don't know. I can't be sure. Cyrinda also came and went throughout the night. She tried to engage me in conversation a few times, but … I can't be sure. It doesn't seem real now. Trina, Ronnie, Cyrinda … all of it. All of this. Nothing is real except Bethy. Not even when Ronnie said something about Barbara meeting us at the motel. That didn't feel real, either. Maybe. I don't know. In my fixed position, with my eyes trained on the kids playing in the backyard of Bethy's house again, I'm not sure if *I'm* even real.

I shake my head back and forth to jiggle that thought from my head because everything that has happened to me has brought me to this moment, and I am determined to shine just as brightly as Bethy. I've watched, observed, and learned from everything that Ronnie has done for Barbara. I've witnessed time and time again the failure of the rituals, heard the disappointment in Barbara's voice, saw the tears of the twins in the drawing when they realized it wasn't their time to be reborn. But as I watch Bethy from the window, I know that will all come to an end very soon.

Suddenly, as if she heard my thoughts, Bethy stops running around in her backyard and lifts her face to my window. She sees me! I know she does! Her head tilts curiously from side to side as if she's trying to decipher what it is she sees. Does *she* see *me* shining back at her? Can she recognize the light inside of *me*? I swivel my head to check the room, to make sure I am alone. I raise my hand to the glass in a feeble wave, and Bethy glows magnificently like she's smiling and waving back. A rush of energy overtakes me. A wave of warmth churns in my chest and makes my fingertips numb.

She sees me!

I smile back, trying to project my spirit, my soul, my own beautiful energy onto her. She puts her hands over her eyes, then takes them away. *Peek-a-boo.* Such a primitive game for an innocent child. But, she's playing with me, so I return the peek-a-boo gestures, and in sync with each other, our lights, our auras go flashing wildly. I once learned in a psychology class that when little children cover their faces, or hide behind something, or put a blanket over their head, or even close their eyes, they truly believe that they disappear and can't be seen. I always thought that to be so odd, but then again, it makes sense because a young child's brain is still so very underdeveloped. Bethy can't be more than two years old, and the gaggle of kids in the yard with her—her siblings, I presume—are varied in their ages. I count seven who don't shine. They pay Bethy no mind as they race past her and around her, in and out of the back door to the house, and recklessly climb the big tree on the property. Like, it feels like they are all aware that Bethy is there but are all very lax in that awareness. Bethy is a good girl. A pure girl. She doesn't fuss at her brothers and sisters or whine or cry to be picked up or coddled. She's a content toddler who knows how to play a mean game of Peek-a-boo!

My stomach groans, but not in a hungry sort of way. It's like my body is missing something. There's a vacancy in my soul. A want. A longing. A desire for the uncontaminated light. I need to find a way to draw her out, to draw her to me. I remember Ronnie bringing food into the room before, so I shift my eyes to the little table, and just as I had suspected, there's a Hershey's Bar sticking out of the brown paper bag. All kids love candy, right? So, I swivel my arm to the table and grab it, and I hold it up to the window, hoping to catch Bethy's attention. Her light flashes like a strobe, and I know the vision of the candy excites her. It excites me too. My stomach roars again. Still not with hunger.

I grab the bottle of pop and candy, leave the room, and make my way to the shrubbery that separates the back of the motel with the back of Beth's yard. "Bethy!" I whisper forcefully so as to get her attention, but not alert her siblings. "Bethy!" I say again, waving the candy in between the bushes.

She sees me from the back steps of the house and trudges over. Her brown curls bounce wildly as she shuffles her little legs. Left foot. Right foot. Bounce. Bounce. Bounce. The others don't notice her wandering to the bushes, or maybe they do and just don't suspect anything is amiss. They don't sense the predator descending on the pack. For a split second, my heart hurts so bad because I don't want to be a predator. I'm not like Ronnie in that respect, and Bethy is so sweet and innocent that it pains me to think of any harm coming her way. But her light… that mesmerizing light… it's intoxicating, and I know Barbara needs it. She can use it. Cultivate it. Exploit it. And bring about the new world that she promised.

"Hi, Bethy," I say when she gets close enough.

"Hi," she says bashfully in her sweet little voice.

"You want to go take a walk with me?"

She nods her head, and her curls fluff up around her head.

"Groovy!" I exclaim. "We can go to the park and have some fun. Would you like that?"

She nods again, and I outstretch my arm beckoning her to me.

Gingerly, she eases her way between the bushes and grabs my hand. I am amazed at how trusting she is. But I guess most children that age are. Most children rely on the integrity and good intentions of the adults around them for they know nothing else. Or maybe my light spoke to her light, and it makes her feel safe and loved. *Her* light makes *me* feel safe and loved, and when she wraps her tiny fingers around mine, her energy shoots up my arm, and I am saturated in a wave of peace.

I look around to make sure the other children are unaware of the situation, and when I see that the coast is clear, I clutch her tightly and scurry behind the shrubs and into the parking lot. "Come on, sweetie, let me pick you up," I say, and she lifts her free arm up in the air. Instinctively, I scoop her up and press her tightly to my chest and begin the trot across the motel parking lot and sneak clandestinely through the tree-lined neighborhood.

The river calls to me. To Bethy. Even though it's a few blocks away, it roars in my head like a song. Like the song in Trent's car and the song in Barbara's house. Music without a name. And I think maybe it wasn't ever really music that I was hearing after all. Maybe it was the song of the Mississippi River this whole time singing my name. Making sure I would get to this very moment in time.

"My name is Trixie," I sing. "And you're Bethy, aren't you?"

"Lilbeth," she corrects.

"Elizabeth?" I question, and she nods. "But they all call you Bethy, don't they?" I smile wide and unassuming. She smiles back. "You have a lot of brothers and sisters, don't you, Bethy?"

"Yeah!" she yells out like the excited child she is.

"You're the baby, aren't you?"

"I not a baby," she pouts.

"Oh? How old are you?"

She tucks her head against the crook of my shoulder and holds up two fingers.

"Two?" I exclaim in mock surprise. "Well, you're definitely not a baby. You're such a big girl! A big, smart, and very pretty girl!"

She softly giggles against my neck.

"Oh, we are going to have so much fun!" I say, adjusting her small body on my hip. "When we get to the river, we'll have candy and play games. We're gonna have a super fun time, just you and me. 'Cause I'm bright and you're bright, and we have lights that want to play together."

She relaxes against me, almost melting into me. Sweat beads form on my forehead and underneath Bethy's shirt where my hand secures her. It's hot out. Sweltering.

Must be eighty-four degrees, I hear a voice call out. I can't make out whose it is, but it reminds me of broken glass crunching under a tire in the movie theatre parking lot, and for some weird reason, I immediately think of Arrah. A voice like glass from the pop bottle smashing on the ground.

Don't break it, a young boy's voice says.

How is she even carrying that kid? a young girl chimes.

The twins. Gretchen and David. They speak to me through Arrah. Clear as bells. Clear as day. I am disoriented and shift Bethy again from one side to the other.

I feel a weight in my chest as my vision blurs. The river roars. Bellows. Shrieks to me as I get closer. As we get closer. Me, Bethy, Gretchen, David, Arrah, and all the other heksas I saw when I was initiated. Singing. Laughing. Song of the ancients! I was initiated! 'Cause I'm a witch doing witchy shit. No, not yet. I am still only an acolyte. An associate. An integral part of a larger design. But soon I will manifest my true being. For I am loyal to the Church of Barbara. I am loyal to the Crimson Coven. I will see this through even if I have to wear Ronnie-colored glasses. My hands are numb from holding the child so tightly. So tightly. Down to the river. Slick hands of sweat and blood with tingling fingertips. Clenching a glass bottle. But don't break it.

Wind blows off from the strong currents of the water providing a temporary relief from the hot summer sun. I stare into the deep channel of the water imagining the chasm beneath. How far does it go down? Where does it end? What's at the bottom of the mighty Mississippi? I grip Bethy tighter because I'm afraid if she wiggles loose, she might trip and stumble into the water and would never be seen again. Then her light would go out for good, and I would have missed my chance to harvest it for myself. She squirms a little but quickly quiets down when I squeeze her.

Like most kids, I'd dreamed of running away my entire life. There was nothing I wanted more than to escape and be free from the constant verbal and physical abuse I endured on a daily basis. How pathetic my lot in life—my real parents didn't want me. I was just a nuisance to them. Easily discarded. And the foster families who took me in over the years didn't really want me either. It looked good on paper for them to have me, but when it was all said and done, I was a burden, another mouth to feed. Patricia the unwanted. Trixie the lost little girl who no one cared for. Yeah, the trick was on Trixie, alright!

When I did finally get the courage to run away, I ran straight into the open arms of Barbara, and I don't think I've ever felt more loved, and wanted, and needed in my entire life. Even my static with Ronnie has proven to be a real, actual relationship. I imagine that is how blood sisters interact when they are vying for the attention of a parent. Blood sisters. Acolytes. Don't break the glass.

I think about what Cyrinda said yesterday—about how she's planning on going back to Indiana, back to where we came from. It hurts me to imagine us being separated because she's been such an integral part of my life. She's always been by my side, to my right. She's always been the shadow to my light. Well, I guess she no longer wants to be there—in the shadow. Maybe it's her time to be free too. I knew she wouldn't have the stomach for the path I've chosen. I knew she wouldn't have the fortitude to face her fears and conquer the old demons of the past in order to make way for the new. For the what's to come. For the here. For the now. For the nowhere. 'Cause I saw that rip in the sky, and I felt what was beyond. And to think of the new world that Barbara wants to create excites me. It excites me to no end. She promised me a place in it. She promised I have a role to play. And that alone is enough to drive me to the river. To the good ole Mississippi with child in arms listening to the roar of the water and the roar of my stomach, and the voices in the mist and the song in my head, and Gretchen and David bickering over who's going to arrive first, and Arrah's crunchy glass-voice scraping on the side of Bethy's neck, and the rush of Ronnie's murderous essence filling in my lungs, and Cyrinda's face blinking in and out of my memory, and runes, and blood, and fire, and screams, and a five-pointed star drawn in concrete, and a song with no music, and a hand on my knee, and Clark asking about June but June is dead dead dead, and a missing person's flyer with all the names of all the girls with all the *visions of burning sinners and devils with visions of burning sinners and devils with visions of burning sinners and devils...*

It's completely dark out when I stumble back to the motel room alone. My jeans are ripped at the knees exposing my scraped-up skin. The flesh is shredded on each kneecap—red and swollen with just a speckle of blood dots that bloomed on the surface but never spilled. At some point in time, I must have fallen somewhere or gotten into some kind of scuffle, but I can't remember. Ronnie opens the door violently and quickly pulls me into the pitch-black room. Barbara jumps up from the bed to greet me.

"Where the fuck have you been?" Ronnie scolds. Even though she tempers the volume of her voice, I can hear the anger in her words.

"I… I was out," I stammer, still trying to piece together where I was or what I had been doing.

"Out?" she squawks. "Are you kidding me right now?"

Bright flashing lights from outside illuminate the room, and I automatically think that maybe Bethy is outside in her backyard running around. *But that's impossible.* The lights that shine through are red and blue and pulsate in a rhythmic fashion, and I immediately sense the artificial essence of them.

"What's all that?" I ask absently.

"All that is a whole lotta trouble for us," Ronnie says as she nods her head in the direction of the window. "They've been at it for a few hours looking for someone. A kid, I think." She looks to Barbara, "If the fuzz start nosing around here or at the lake and trace us back to…"

Suddenly, it dawns on me that Barbara has made her way to Cape Girardeau. I don't know when and I don't know how, but she's here in the hotel room. I stir with excitement from just being in her presence.

"Relax, Rhonda," Barbara says calmly. "I told you; everything is taken care of. You have nothing to worry about. We're not going back to the Salem house. We're done with all that."

Panic rises in my chest. "Not going home to Salem?"

"It's okay, Trixie. It was time to relocate anyway. We'll be fine. This isn't something I haven't done before."

Ronnie runs her fingers through her black, slicked-back hair. "I think it might be time to relocate *now*, Barbara," she urges, her voice becoming desperate and concerned.

Barbara glances out the window and assesses the activity behind the motel. She narrows her eyes for a second and her expression makes me uneasy. "Hmmm," she tries to sing in a soothing voice. "You might be right."

"Wait!" I protest and hold up the glass pop bottle. "I want to show you this."

Ronnie huffs and rolls her eyes. "Really, Trix? We don't have time for…"

But Barbara's eyes go large when she catches a glimpse of it. I know she sees it. I know she sees the light glowing from inside the bottle. Ronnie can't because Ronnie is just an acolyte. But Barbara can, and so can I, so maybe that means I'm just a little bit more…

"Where did you…" Barbara mumbles in a faraway voice. Her eyes glaze over, and she extends her arm, practically begging me to give her the bottle.

"What are you talking about?" Ronnie says, confused. But Barbara ignores her. I ignore her. Barbara and I are locked in to each other and to the bottle, and no one else exists, and nothing else matters.

"I know it's not much, but…"

"Where did you get this?" Barbara says, cutting me off.

"I found it. I found it for you." The words sound so stupid, so dumb, but it's the only response I can offer.

Barbara takes the bottle from me and holds it up in front of her face. The light from within illuminates her visage, makes her alabaster skin shine like a thousand suns. Flashing against her skin are the outlines of the runes—on her cheeks, her forehead, tip of her nose, and chin—like the light is revealing the words that dwell hidden underneath her. Words that are always there but can never be seen. I wonder if I held the bottle against her entire body, would the runes appear with the light of the contents within? Of course they would. For Barbara is the truth and the light and the way.

"Did I do good?" I ask.

"Oh, sweet, sweet Trixie," she moans. "This is more than good."

Chapter Eighteen

Monday, June 14th 1965
The Downtowner Motel
Morgan Oak Street, Cape Girardeau, Missouri
Early Morning of the Full Moon

It's mesmerizing the way the contents in the bottle alters the very essence of Barbara's being. Like how the colors in her eyes flash wildly like lights from a siren. The actual police lights fill the room with red and blue, but Barbara's eyes are much, much brighter. She and I sit on the edge of the bed staring at the bottle between us. The curves and edges in the glass bend the light within, and it sparkles and dazzles in the darkness of the room.

Ronnie paces back and forth across the floor trying to avoid being seen at the window. I know she doesn't see what Barbara sees in the bottle—what I see in the bottle. If she did, her focus would be aligned with ours, rather than the commotion on the outside. Nervously, she wipes her hands down the sides of her jeans and slaps the empty pockets. "C'mon, man!" she says to the both of us. "It's getting pretty hairy out there! It's just a matter of time before they start knocking on these doors, Barbara. We need to split! Like now!"

I know there are voices outside. I can discern that much. Voices yell for "Bethy!" and "Elizabeth!" in frantic, ear-splitting tones, but it sounds muted to me. Faraway. So distant that it's coming from another place and time.

"Ronnie, be cool," Barbara says calmly waving her hand in the air.

"Be cool? Be cool? The fuzz is right outside our back door. They're looking for some lost kid. Maybe for Trina too. Who knows? But I know they're going to be here, like, any second and you want me to be cool?" She panics, and rightfully so. If this had been any other time, any other place, I probably would have panicked too. With Cyrinda around, I definitely would have had to calm her down. Speaking of Cyrinda... I can scarcely remember when I saw her last, and she isn't here right now. Maybe she left? Maybe she high tailed it out of here and back to Indiana? Maybe she's dead in a ditch somewhere? Maybe she's just *gone*? And honestly, would it be so bad if now was the time of our parting? She doesn't need to see this. She doesn't need to be a part of any of this. As much as it pains me, I know that she and I need to go our separate ways. It's time.

"The police are not coming over," Barbara asserts, interrupting my thoughts. "Nobody is. At least not yet. They can't even see the motel."

Ronnie's face screws up. "What do you mean? Of course they can see the…"

"You glamoured us," I say knowingly to Barbara, and she closes her eyes and gives me a small nod.

Like pulling a chain on a basement light, Ronnie snaps out of her fear and kneels down beside Barbara. Because, as much as Ronnie doesn't know, Ronnie *knows*. She's believed in Barbara, trusted Barbara, and followed Barbara for almost a year now. She's done things for her and with her, and she knows what Barbara is capable of—of the power she wields. They have a relationship like no other, that I can't deny. Her entire demeanor shifts as she places her hands on top of Barbara's knees. Her voice levels out to her natural, smooth timbre, and something in her transforms back to the Ronnie who first greeted me at the Salem house front door. "How long do we have?"

"I'm not sure," Barbara answers. "I'm hoping long enough to do *this*." She raises her eyebrows in the direction of the bottle.

Ronnie's eyes dart from the bottle back to me with a suspicious glance. "We don't have any blood bags with us, Barbara. They're all back in Salem."

"I know," Barbara agrees.

"What's in that bottle isn't nearly enough," Ronnie continues.

"I know," Barbara repeats, then glances at me.

This time, Ronnie's eyebrows raise. "The full moon was yesterday, though."

"No," I interject. "It's actually now. Tonight. I mean, this morning. I mean…"

"Trixie's right," Barbara says. "Now is perfect."

Ronnie's face darkens and she narrows her eyes at me as if she were shooting darts at my head. "It still won't be enough. Unless you're suggesting that…"

"No!" Barbara replies. "I'm not suggesting anything like that."

"Anything like *what*?" I exclaim.

"We'll have to improvise a little," she continues, ignoring my outburst. "But with this," she holds up the bottle in the air, "and her…" she tips the bottle in my direction, "I think it could work."

"Wait!" I shout, and Ronnie quickly *shushes* me. "Wait," I repeat, lowering my voice. "What do you mean 'and her?'"

Barbara stands up from the bed and retrieves her ceremonial knife from the nightstand. "Nothing too crazy, I promise. Just a little bit of your blood."

Something in me tenses up for a split second, but she kisses the top of my forehead, and the kiss washes any fear away.

"Come," she beckons, so I rise and follow her and Ronnie to the bathroom.

Barbara places the knife on the countertop, hands the bottle to me, and undresses as Ronnie turns the water on to fill the tub. Barbara whispers something inaudible, something I don't understand. I know they are words, and in some way, I know what they mean, but they are so very foreign to me. My ears think they hear the words 'sacrifice' and 'reckoning' and 'rebirth' and 'beginning,' but I can't be sure.

But I *am* sure! Because I faintly hear children's voices in the distance. Frantic children's voices calling out to me, screaming what sounds like a warning, an admonition. It's the twins. Gretchen and David. And there is pain and dread in the message they try to send me. I can't understand what they try to say because their voices are drowned out by the voices of the people outside screaming for "Bethy! Bethy! Bethy!" and the atmosphere in the bathroom is thick with the magic of Barbara's concealment spell and the rushing of the faucet water. I open my mouth to alert Barbara, but something paralyzes me. Something on the inside. Some driving force that takes my breath away—takes my voice away. I couldn't protest the ritual even if I tried.

Barbara submerges her naked body in the water with a long, deep sigh as steam rises from the tub and encircles her like a mystical ghost. Her dense breasts bobble atop the hazy water like two partially submerged white buoys. *Like buoys in the Mississippi.* She points to the knife on the counter with her long, white finger and Ronnie quickly obliges and kneels next to her.

"You are my conduit tonight, Rhonda. I consecrate you as the surrogate to bring about the children. And so, with the blood and the light,

I offer this to you—to mark me with the seal of the Blodheksa, to open me, to fill me with life once again."

Ronnie first takes Barbara's left wrist, and with the athame, she carves a rune into her skin. I shudder at the act because Barbara already has runes on her! I want to scream for Ronnie to stop! "Barbara's runes are just underneath! They're there! I saw them in the light! You don't have to cut her!" But the words can't come out. Ronnie does the same to Barbara's right wrist, and then carves a five-pointed star into the center of Barbara's chest. Barbara doesn't flinch, and I remember what she told me at my initiation ceremony: *The athame will only hurt you if you are not willing to give yourself over one hundred percent. It is very old and has many a song to sing.* By the way Barbara sways her head back and forth, she must hear the music of the blade. There is no pain for her in this trance.

When Ronnie finishes, Barbara dips her arms and upper body fully into the tub and the blood from her wounds turns the water a sheer shade of pink.

"Hold out your arm," Ronnie says from behind me, and I know what she intends to do.

This will not hurt me, this will not hurt me, this will not hurt, I say to myself over and over again as she drags the blade down the length of my forearm. I watch in awe as my flesh tears open and the blood rises to the surface, but when I hold my arm over the water, I'm shocked to see there is no blood—just a stream of light flows through my veins and into the tub. The tub turns redder, but I can't see actual blood! When my life force commingles with the water and Barbara's blood and her open wounds, her eyes open wide, and she gasps in ecstasy. Like she's awakening. Rising. An orgasmic rush washes through her. Her eyes change color frantically like a supersonic, super-speed kaleidoscope, and her mouth gapes open with short, labored pants. I know that euphoria. It was what I felt when I tasted her blood in the ceremony. But only this time, she's drunk on me—on my life, on my light. Her body spasms at her waist and down to her legs. The tips of her toes peek out from beneath the water and they wiggle excitedly. Barbara's eyes are glazed over. Stuck on the color white. Completely white. Hazy white. No pupils. Just white. She's not on this plane of existence.

"My God! It's working!" Ronnie gushes. "Do you see, Trixie? Look! Look! It's working!" She takes the glass bottle from me and turns the sink on so that the water barely trickles out. She puts the bottle underneath the faucet so that the bottle gets a little drink, and then covers the mouth of it with her hand and shakes it up.

"Why are you doing that?" I ask.

"I know what I'm doing, Trixie. I've worked with blood before. I want to get as much of it out of this bottle as possible," she says matter-of-factly.

Blood? What the hell is she talking about, blood?

"Blood?" I say my inner thoughts.

Her face screws up questioningly. "Um, yeah. Blood. You put it there, didn't you?" she scolds me like I'm some kind of idiot. "You got it from somewhere. From *someone*. And it got Barbara all curious-like and fascinated, so here we are."

My ears get hot with embarrassment. I'm not sure what she's talking about, but I just nod and say, "Oh, yeah, yeah, for sure."

Ronnie nods. "Groovy. Let's get on with it, shall we?"

"But what's that going to do?"

"You know what it's supposed to do, Trixie. Barbara is in the other place right now. You know that tear in the sky. I know you've seen it! She's there, Trixie! She ascended! And she's open right now. This is everything she's always talked about. This is everything she said it would be. Life will create life."

Still, I'm nervous. Still, I'm scared. I don't know fully what the expectation is because there's still so much I don't know. But I do know. But I don't. And now it's real. And now it's happening, and I'm conflicted in my feelings. And I miss Cyrinda. "Far out," I say, giving Ronnie the green light to proceed.

And with that, Ronnie takes the bottle over to the tub and empties the contents onto Barbara's upper body, making sure the blood from the bottle coats the carved-out star on her chest. I hold my breath in anticipation, not knowing what to expect. Ronnie puts the bottle on the edge of the tub and moves over to my side. We hold each other tightly—waiting and watching.

Suddenly, Barbara's body tenses up rigid and stiff. It extends out into the supine position with unnatural jerky movements. Her mouth opens wide like she is screaming, but no sound comes out at first. Ronnie grips me tighter in pure dread when the deep and painful delayed scream finally escapes from Barbara's lips. I put my free hand over my exposed ear to help block out the sound, for it's not just Barbara's scream, it's the painful scream of a thousand voices crying out at once, a thousand tortured heksas across the span of space and time feeling an agonizing sensation all at once, wherever and whenever they are. The sound fills the room, fills the motel, fills the world. It pierces my brain like stabbing needles. Ronnie winces, and I know she feels it too.

"What's happening to her?" I cry out in desperation. "Is she dying? Oh God, Ronnie! She's dying isn't she?"

Barbara's body levitates from the water, but only it's not Barbara. Like her kaleidoscope eyes, her entire essence shifts and turns and changes. The runes that were hidden under her skin (the runes only I could see in the light of the bottle) rush to the surface with an orange glowing light. Like mini flames lighting her up. Lighting her up from the inside out. Burning her up from the inside out. But it's not Barbara! The body before us is a different appearance altogether. A different variation. Barbara, but not. But the Barbara we know blinks in and out of our vision in measured beats. Her hair goes stark white, then back to black, then white again, then black, then white. And the orange and yellow flame runes die out to blackened ash prints all over her, cauterizing the brands that Ronnie previously made. The Barbara-not-Barbara body convulses above the water and foam forms at the sides of her mouth. Barbara-not-Barbara. An ancient being pushing its way through to the present-day woman. *Is this Blodwyn? Is Blodwyn wrestling with Barbara for dominion in this current-day world?*

The room shakes. The motel shakes. The world shakes like an earthquake rising up from the depths of the planet's core. I dig my nails into Ronnie's arms in anticipation of the very building collapsing into a chasm of hot magma.

"Help her! Help her! I scream at Ronnie over the sound of the deafening cry of the witches.

"What did you do, Trixie?" she screams back. "What the fuck did you do?"

She lets go of me and raises her fist.

And everything goes dark when it crashes down on the side of my head.

My groggy eyes struggle to flutter open. The heavy lids can barely open up halfway, and I struggle to focus. Instinctively, I try to bring my hands up to my head to scratch an itch, but I quickly realize they are bound in place. My body jolts, and I am suddenly wrapped in a sense of fear—I don't know where I am, when I am, or how I even got to this place. After a few minutes, I'm able to shake the drugged-up feeling away and open my eyes completely. I'm on a table. In some kind of warehouse or maybe a basement—a place with concrete walls and floor and the smell of mildew and gasoline permeating the air.

"Hello?" I want to yell, but the word is lost in my throat. Maybe from being drugged or being held by a spell? *'Cause I've seen that happen before.* "Cyrinda! Cyrinda! Where are you? I need you!" I want to say, but again, the words are nowhere to be found. I'm so scared, I can't even stand it. Frozen, both literally and metaphorically. I suddenly realize that I need Cyrinda so very badly. I need her to get out of this situation and move on with our lives. *She was right all along.*

And then as if appearing out of nowhere, Ronnie and Barbara manifest in the room with a shadowy figure behind them. "Cyrinda!" I cry out, and this time the word is able to manifest into reality. Ronnie and Barbara give each other a knowing glance as Barbara approaches me. She looks different. Older, somehow. Her long, dark hair now has a thick shock of white going from the top of her forehead all the way down to her waist. She and Ronnie are both dressed in black jeans and black turtleneck sweaters. *Odd for summer*, I think. Ronnie clicks her tongue on the roof of her mouth with a condescending "tsk" sound, and I grimace at her.

"Oh, Trixie," Barbara sings. "So lost and misguided."

"Barbara," I manage to croak. "What happened? What's going on?"

"Sweet girl," she continues. "I had so many plans for us. I had so many dreams."

"The ritual? What happened? I thought you died. Then Ronnie hit me and…"

She moves closer to me and pets my head moving my slick hair off my forehead. It's such a soothing, calming gesture I can almost feel the forgiveness in her fingertips. But then I realize I'm wet. Slippery from head to toe.

"I didn't die," she reassures.

"So, what happened? Did it work?"

"No, dear," she coos. "It unfortunately did not."

"Why?" I cry out. "It *was* working!"

She pets my head again. Her fingers are hot against my skin. "Just exactly where did you get that blood from?" she asks, and like shocks of lightning to my brain I am rocked with images of the bottle, the blood, the light, the Mississippi River, the motel, Cyrinda, Bethy… all of it comes crashing into my head, flash after flash of painful images boring holes into my skull.

I wince from the excruciating pain, and she stops.

"You used a child's blood, didn't you?" Ronnie calls to me. "That's why you were so obsessed with that bitch's kid!"

"I… I… I didn't mean…" I stammer.

"Shhh," Barbara coaxes. "There's an unspoken code among us, Trixie. You must never bring harm to a child. It is forbidden. The Blodsøster and the Blodbrødre are the most special of children, and it is important to respect the innocence of all. But you didn't know that. How could you? It's okay now. I'm okay now. When Ronnie put the child's blood on me, something woke up, and it spoke to me the truth of what I need to do."

My heart sinks when I hear this, and I suddenly realize that I am in grave danger. "Barbara," I beg, "I am so sorry. How can I make it up to you? How can I make it right? Please let me fix this."

"Oh, you will," Ronnie sneers, and Barbara shoots her a wild look then turns back to me with her lovely smile. Her soft smile. Her "everything is gonna be alright" smile.

The figure behind Ronnie moves toward the corner of the room, and I struggle to make out who it is. "Cyrinda? Is that you?" I call out and Ronnie bursts out with a laugh.

"What's so funny?" I yell at her and jerk against my restraints. "You always had a beef with Cyrinda! Why do you hate her so much? You never even got to know her! You barely ever spoke with her!"

Ronnie huffs. "'Cause there's no one to speak *to!*"

I gasp. "What the fuck do you mean by that?"

"Oh, Trixie," Barbara says with her sweet, lulling voice. "You still don't know? Cyrinda isn't real, darling. She's just you. She's just a figment of your imagination."

I squint my eyes to get a better look at the figure behind Ronnie. I see her! It's Cyrinda! Her blonde hair bounces at her shoulders. A yellow duffle bag flung across her back. Her eyes wide with love and friendship. She's here! What is Barbara talking about? Cyrinda is my bestest friend in the whole wide world. She's been with me through thick and thin. Through good times and bad. Through rain and fire. Through one failed family after the next. What does she mean she's not real? She's standing right there, walking right towards me!

Barbara starts humming a song. A familiar song. "Me and My Shadow." And as Cyrinda gets closer, her body disintegrates from the bottom up into a plume of shadowy smoke. Right before my eyes. She gives me one last wave and smile and then the shadows swallow her whole, and she's gone.

I shut my eyes tightly in disbelief at what I saw. It can't be true. It can't be. "You're lying!" I scream with everything in me.

But I'm not, Barbara says directly into my mind.

Confused, the tears stream down my face. My heart feels like it's going to leap out of my chest and do a tap dance on my stomach. I feel like I'm spinning. Or the room's spinning. Did I kill that little girl? Where am I? Who am I? Where do I belong? What is happening? Cyrinda's not real?

Did I kill Cyrinda? Is this even real life? How did I get here?

"Easy, easy," Barbara says as she wipes the tears from my cheeks.

She is so soft and sweet and comforting. I take big gulps of gasoline-smelling air, but the fumes are making me lightheaded, and I can't see straight, and I…

"It's okay, Trixie. Patricia Bluebell McGovern. I know what I have to do. I know what *you* have to do. You are a part of me. A part of *us*. You always were and you always will be, and your name will be carried on, and the bravery of your sacrifice will never be forgotten. I know this is all so sudden, but it's been in the stars since you were born. You were destined for this moment, Trixie. Destined for the now and here."

Her words slow my heartbeat. Her voice soothes my anxiety and terror. "The nowhere?" I mumble.

"Yes. But the nowhere is everywhere. And soon we will be all at once. Please know that you are needed and loved. I need you, Trixie. The twins need you. It is your sacrifice that will be the catalyst for their rebirth. You are still pure, darling. You did not kill that girl, and therefore you remain innocent. And your innocence preserved will be my key. For you are one with the Crimson Coven."

I smile. I'm okay. It's okay. I know the truth, and I can move on knowing I played my part for a larger design. For once I am needed. For once I am loved.

"I am the Crimson Coven," I say.

Barbara kisses my forehead. Her lips are so hot it burns my skin. I feel its heat all throughout my body as the smoke from the pyre wafts up into my nostrils. I close my eyes and smile. Cyrinda's faded face stays in my mind, and I happily relax. I'll be with her soon.

"You are the Witch of the Crimson Coven," I hear a voice say before the roar of the flames overcomes me.

Book Club Questions

1. Cyrinda and Trixie are foster kids, an unlikely background for our main characters. Why might Trent have been so attracted to them? And why Trixie specifically?

2. The book is set in the 1960s, a decade often labeled "the years of hope, days of rage." What significance, if any, can you apply to the Crimson Coven?

3. In chapter 4, Cyrinda tells Trixie, "Your roots are coming in." She referred to her hair, but given the context of the story, what else might she have meant?

4. There is something both real and unreal about movies. How does Trixie's job parallel her journey with the Coven?

5. What do you think Trixie means when she refers to Cyrinda as "me and my shadow?"

6. Why does Trixie care so much about her usefulness to Barbara?

7. Much of the story takes place in the spring. Is there any significance to this amid Trixie's journey?

8. Trixie says she needs the little girl Bethy because of the light in her, but it borders on obsession. Could there be anything else contributing to that obsession besides the light?

9. What is your reaction to the ending?

10. Trixie mentions hippies a few times and seems to dislike them and their drugs. What irony, if any, can you find in that?

11. Who is the true villain of this story?

12. If you have read any of the other books in the series, how does this one compare and contrast with those?

Author Bio

Maria DeVivo writes horror and dark fantasy for both YA and adult audiences. Each of her series has been Amazon best-sellers and has won multiple awards since 2012. A lover of all things dark and demented, the worlds she creates are fantastical and immersive. Get swept away in the lands of elves, zombies, angels, demons, and witches (but not all in the same place). Maria takes great pleasure in warping the comfort factor in her readers' minds—just when you think you've reached a safe space in her stories, she snaps you back into her twisted reality.

Discover more at
4HorsemenPublications.com

10% off using HORSEMEN10